"I'm doing my best to leave town, you know."

"I know." Rachel brought her eyes back to Matt's face and gave him a sad smile. "And I'm not stopping you."

"As long as I can do well with the presentation to the schoolkids tomorrow, I'm pretty sure I've got the job."

"Congratulations." She forced a smile and nodded quickly. "You deserve it."

"I'm not as excited as I thought I'd be."

"No?" She tried to force some cheerfulness, but failed. "I'm sorry. You're my first friend here in town, and I'm going to miss you."

"Me, too." He sighed. "If things were different—"

"You don't have to say it," she said quietly. "It's okay. They aren't different."

Rachel couldn't help the melancholy thoughts that rose up inside her. She thought of her husband, who'd died too soon, of her son whose birth mother hadn't been able to care for him, of her attempts to rebuild a life for her little boy, and now of Matt who had wormed his way into her life, and who would be off to new adventures just as soon as he could manage it. She felt lonely standing there, because no matter how solid an̶̶̶̶̶̶̶̶̶̶̶̶ now, this wouldn't l̶

Patricia Johns willfully became a starving artist after she finished her BA in English literature. She lived in a tiny room in the downtown core of a city, worked sundry part-time jobs to keep herself fed and wrote the first novel she would have published. That was over ten years and ten novels ago. She's now married with a young son, and always has a new book on the go.

Books by Patricia Johns

Love Inspired

His Unexpected Family
The Rancher's City Girl
A Firefighter's Promise

A Firefighter's Promise

Patricia Johns

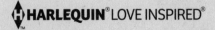

HARLEQUIN LOVE INSPIRED®

LOVE INSPIRED BOOKS

Recycling programs
for this product may
not exist in your area.

ISBN-13: 978-0-373-87960-1

A Firefighter's Promise

www.Harlequin.com

Printed in U.S.A.

He makes me lie down in green pastures, He leads
me beside quiet waters, He restores my soul.
—*Psalms* 23:2–3

To Deputy Fire Chief Tim, our own hometown hero.

And of course, I dedicate this book to
my husband, who inspires the romantic in me.
He still makes my heart race.

Chapter One

Rachel Carter licked her finger and wiped a smear of chocolate from her son's cheek. He squirmed away from her and made a face.

"Mom, stop it," he complained.

"Stand still, Christopher." She pulled a tissue out of her jeans pocket to finish the job. "Are you ready?"

The boy twisted around to look at the firehouse. "This is it?"

Rachel's gaze flickered past her son's face to the two-story brick building. Old-fashioned brickwork surrounded three large garage doors, and a row of windows stretched across the second story. July sunlight filtered through the rustling leaves of two spreading oak trees, dappling the broad drive. From high in the branches, a squirrel chattered down at them, and Rachel paused and looked up, searching for the noisy critic.

Rachel had spent more than enough time at a firehouse like this one back in Billings. From Christmas dinners up in the barracks when her husband had to work over the holidays to quick visits over his long shifts and having to stand back and let him dash off into danger when that siren whooped. She treasured the memories of her late husband, but firehouses didn't bring back pleasant memories for her. It was a demanding job, and not even halfway glamorous for the families of the men and women who put their lives on the line for their communities.

"This is it." She tucked the tissue back into her pocket and regarded her son's pensive face. "This is *your* firehouse, Chris."

"Will the fireman remember me?"

"You're pretty hard to forget, sweetheart." She slid a hand over his rumpled blond curls, and he rewarded her with a grin. "Okay, let's go."

Angling around the side of the building, Rachel found the main entrance, which faced a small parking lot. She pulled open the door and was met with a welcome blast of air-conditioning. A middle-aged woman sat behind the reception desk, and she looked up with a pencil tucked behind one ear and a distracted smile.

"Can I help you?" she asked.

Rachel tucked an errant strand of dark hair back into her ponytail and scooped up Christopher's hand in hers. "Hi, I'm Rachel Carter. We're here to see Captain Matthew Bailey."

"Captain?" The woman raised an eyebrow. "That's Deputy Fire Chief Matthew Bailey."

"Oh." Rachel nodded, registering the higher position. "Is he here?"

The woman narrowed her eyes. "Do you have an appointment, miss?"

Rachel shook her head. "No. I tried calling a few times, but I never did hear back from him."

The receptionist didn't look impressed with her excuse, and Rachel didn't entirely blame her. The security in a firehouse was tight, military-style, and no one just squeezed in.

"The deputy fire chief is a very busy man—" the woman behind the desk began.

A throat cleared to the side and Rachel turned to see a tall man with sandy-blond hair, a tinge of gray at the temples. A pressed navy blue uniform tapered down from wide shoulders to a trim waist, and his dark gaze swept over her as he shot her a lazy grin. Warmth rose in her cheeks.

"What can I do for you, ma'am?"

"Are you—" she paused, adjusting her mind to his new title, and firmly putting his good looks aside "—Deputy Fire Chief—"

"Matt Bailey." He held out a broad, calloused hand.

"I'm Rachel Carter, and this is my son, Chris."

Christopher stared up at the deputy chief, eyes wide. He pressed his lips together into a thin line. He moved a couple of inches closer to Rachel's side, but his eyes were pinned to the tall firefighter.

"Nice to meet you." Matt clasped her hand in a brief handshake. "You're looking for me?" He regarded her in mild curiosity.

"I am, but it's a little bit delicate. Is there somewhere we could talk?"

The receptionist raised her penciled eyebrows and leaned forward in unveiled interest, but Matt gestured down a short hallway. A few office doors opened up on either side, and Rachel tugged her son along with her. Matt's polished shoes clicked against the tile floor, and he stopped at a doorway, glancing back at them with a casual smile.

"Come on in." He gestured them inside, and as she passed him, the musky scent of his cologne tickled her nose.

The room was small and neat, consisting of not much more than a desk and a few file cabinets. Christopher sank into a chair, his gaze locked on the big man, and Rachel remained standing. Matt looked down at the boy thoughtfully, then shifted his attention to Rachel.

"What can I do for you, ma'am?"

"Seven years ago, a baby was dropped off on the doorstep of this firehouse." Rachel's hand fluttered toward her son's shoulder. "We were told that Captain Matthew Bailey was the one who found him."

"Yes, I did find a baby a few years back." His gaze moved back to Christopher and he cleared his throat.

"This is him," Rachel said. "My husband and I adopted Christopher shortly after Social Services picked him up."

"Oh, I see." Matt nodded several times. "Hi, buddy."

"Hi." Christopher eyed the big man uncertainly. "You don't recognize me?"

"It's been a while." A smile flickered at the corners of Matt's lips. "You're a lot bigger now."

Christopher nodded. "I guess."

"So you came to see the firehouse?" Matt asked.

"We came to see you, actually." Rachel straightened her shoulders. Was she completely out of line doing this? She wasn't even sure. "Christopher has wanted to meet the firefighter who found him for a long time now. I've tried calling but never seemed to get through. I'm sorry to just drop in on you like this, but Chris was hoping to meet you."

"Well." Matt's tone turned formal. "It's all part of

the job, Christopher. As a firefighter, I'm here to help the community, and that might be in a fire or at an accident, or even calling Social Services to pick up a baby."

Pick up a baby. Rachel glanced down at her son, not missing the disappointed slump in his small shoulders.

"Did you want to ask Mr. Bailey anything, Christopher?" she prompted hopefully.

Christopher shook his head and looked down.

"But you remember Christopher?" Rachel turned a pleading gaze onto the man before her. She understood his job better than he probably realized, but a little boy mattered more than whatever meetings and paperwork awaited him, and she wasn't going to let this slide by so easily.

"Do I remember you, buddy? Absolutely. It's not every day that a baby gets dropped on our doorstep. Here is an interesting bit of trivia for you. Did you know that firehouses have become a safe place for mothers to drop—" He stopped and cleared his throat again.

Unwanted infants. At least he'd stopped himself. Rachel stared at the deputy fire chief as silence stretched awkwardly between them. Capping the rising irritation inside her, she smiled coolly.

"Do you think Christopher could look at the fire trucks for a couple of minutes while we talk alone?" she asked.

Matt nodded. "Sure." A firefighter crossed the open doorway and Matt rose to his feet. "Johnson!" Was that a hint of desperation in his voice?

The man turned back. "Yes, sir?"

"Would you mind showing this young man the fire trucks for about five minutes?"

"Sure thing, sir."

Christopher looked toward Rachel for permission and she smiled reassuringly. "Go ahead, honey. I won't be long."

Christopher left the room, the firefighter's voice echoing down the hall as he explained some details about the trucks they'd see shortly, and Rachel turned around and shot the deputy chief a withering look. Matt's eyes widened in surprise.

"A little bit of trivia?" She shook her head in exasperation. "He's barely seven years old."

"Yes..." Matt didn't seem to know how to answer that declaration.

"Look, I get that we just kind of dropped in on you, and I can appreciate how awkward this is." She sucked in a breath. "I just want you to know that this really matters to Chris. He really latched on to the story of how you found him. My husband was a firefighter, too, so the whole firefighting thing is pretty important in our family."

"I didn't realize you're married to a firefighter. Is he retired?" Matt asked.

"No, he died in the line of duty."

Matt scrubbed his hands over his face and heaved a sigh. "What happened to him?"

"He was run down by a drunk driver when he was hooking up hoses to put out a fire at an accident." She brushed a wisp of hair off her forehead. "Chris was two at the time, so he doesn't remember him."

"What was his name?"

"Ed Carter."

He nodded slowly. "I remember reading about his passing. That was in Billings, right? I'm really sorry, Mrs. Carter."

"Thank you." She softened her tone. "It was a hard time. That's part of the job, isn't it?" She couldn't help the tremor of anger that rose up inside her when she thought about her husband's death. She knew that he was a hero for his sacrifice, but it didn't change that he'd left a young family behind who still needed him.

"I guess so." His blue eyes met hers and held her gaze for a long moment. "I'm sorry about how I handled this with your son. I'm not good with kids."

"Kids can be a handful," she agreed quietly. She knew that better than anyone. "But my son is a little more complicated than others."

"Oh?"

"He'd been fighting at school, and he was only in the first grade. It had gotten so bad that he was expelled. Our family counselor in Billings suggested that I bring him here to explore his roots, as it were. He's searching for something, and I need to help him find it."

"You think I'm part of that?"

Suddenly it seemed as though she was asking too much. Matthew Bailey didn't know her, or her husband. He didn't owe them anything, and if Chris was struggling, it certainly wasn't his problem. She grimaced.

"I'm sorry. This isn't your problem, and I should be—"

"I didn't say that." His eyes locked on to hers and he dipped his head down slightly to keep the eye contact. "This matters a lot to your little boy."

Rachel let out a pent-up breath. "Yes."

"I wish you'd given me a bit of notice." There was a smile tugging at his lips again, and the heat rose in her cheeks.

"I called three times and left messages, but I didn't

hear back from you," she attempted to explain. She shouldn't have brought Chris here without making an appointment—that was a mistake. She was normally more cautious and planned than this.

"We've got a new receptionist." He shrugged. "It's been…interesting around here."

They were both silent for a long moment, and Rachel attempted to keep her mind away from this firefighter's rugged good looks. She'd been married to a firefighter already, and she knew better than to go down that road again. But she was here, and she'd already trampled all over every polite boundary—

"I hope this isn't too much to ask, but would you be willing to talk to Christopher a little bit?" Rachel hesitated, then plunged on. "I don't mean about the fighting, just about—" she shrugged "—finding him, that sort of thing. I know that my husband wasn't part of your firehouse, but—I'd appreciate this a lot."

Matt was silent for a beat, then nodded.

"I could try, but I should warn you that I'm not the smoothest guy with kids. There is another firefighter who was there that night who might be a better guy to talk to Christopher. He has four kids of his own and he just seems to connect with children better than I do."

Rachel's gaze trailed around the small, impersonal office. There was more to the story—the part where she'd failed her son, too. She hadn't wanted to tell this part. In fact, she'd hoped that a little visit with Christopher's firefighter would be the beginning of some healing. She hadn't counted on Matthew Bailey having his own complications.

"I didn't tell Christopher that he was adopted right

away," Rachel confessed. "I knew I was supposed to, but when Ed died, it blindsided me and I never could find the right moment, or the right words. Last year he asked me about being inside my tummy, and I had to tell him the truth. It was really hard for him." She sighed. "When I told him about you and how you'd found him and held him, that seemed to comfort him a lot. So I told him the story about being found on your doorstep quite often."

"You might have made me into more of a hero than I really am," he said.

"Maybe," she agreed with an apologetic smile. "But he's a kid who needs a hero. And right about now, you fit the bill."

"How long are you in town?" he asked, his tone low and warm.

"For good," she replied with a quick nod. "I've just been hired at the Broxton Park Elementary School to teach the fourth grade."

He froze, dropped his gaze, then cleared his throat. "It opens again this year."

"Yes, I'd read that there was a fire, and this year it will reopen. I'm really grateful for the opportunity. I have family here in Haggerston, and it will be good for Chris to be closer to relatives."

He didn't answer for a long moment, and there seemed to be complicated emotions flickering behind those steely eyes, a hint at what lay behind that granite mask.

"And if I can return the favor, I will," she added quickly. "Here is my phone number and address." She pulled a slip of paper out of her purse and slid it across the desk. "If there is anything I can do... Maybe you have some children in your family who need to be tutored or perhaps I can be of some assistance to the fire department when it comes to school groups or—"

The phone rang and Rachel clamped her mouth shut. Matt picked up the call. He averted his gaze as he spoke quietly, too low for her to make out the words. After a moment, he hung up and shot her an apologetic smile.

"I'm sorry, but I've got a meeting."

Rachel hitched her purse up on her shoulder and nodded quickly. This was getting more and more awkward by the minute, and all she wanted to do right now was to retreat. "Of course. I know that you're busy and I'm grateful for squeezing me in. Thank you for your time, Deputy—"

"Matt."

She blinked. "Pardon me?"

"Call me Matt. And I'm not trying to get rid of you. Maybe we could talk more later. I might be able to take you up on your offer, too."

Rachel's cheeks grew warmer. "I'm glad. And thank you."

"My pleasure."

He reached out a hand and enveloped her slender fingers in his warm grip. A shadow darkened the doorway, and Rachel stepped back to allow the man entrance.

As she slipped from the small office, she glanced back and found Matt's warm gaze locked on her over his visitor's shoulder. A smile flickered over his lips and he turned his attention back toward the gentleman in his office. Rachel smothered a sigh and turned her steps in the direction her son had gone. This wasn't going to be as simple as she'd hoped.

* * *

As the petite dark-haired woman disappeared down the hallway, Matt closed his office door. She was persistent—he'd give her that. She was also one of them—the widow of a firefighting brother, and he couldn't just forget about that. Firefighters were a tight group. When you put your own life on the line, you had to trust your brothers to step up and take care of your family if the worst-case scenario happened.

Which had happened for Ed Carter, God rest his soul. He remembered that death clearly because it had been so pointless. The firefighter had been hooking up hoses in order to fight a fire on a rolled tanker when a drunk driver careened by and took him out. Death in a fire seemed more acceptable, somehow, than the way Ed Carter had died, and it felt strange to know that he'd just met Firefighter Carter's widow.

She's beautiful.

This wasn't exactly the thought that was appropriate for a time like this, and he pushed it back and turned his attention to his visitor.

The portly gentleman settled himself in the visitor's chair without much room to spare. He was an older man with gray, thinning hair and red cheeks.

"It's good to meet you, Matthew." The older man adjusted himself and shot Matt a grandfatherly smile.

"Likewise. It's nice to put a face to the voice, Mr. Bernard."

"This is the less formal part of the process. Don't think of this as an interview—it's more of a meet and greet." He held out a business card.

"Understood." Matt accepted the card and scanned

the details. He wasn't fooled, though. This was most certainly an interview.

"I sit on the South Maitland city hiring committee," Mr. Bernard explained. "I'm just here to get to know you a little bit. I want to see your style, what you've done here in Haggerston."

"My pleasure." Matt leaned back in his chair.

"You've applied to be fire chief in South Maitland," he went on. "And obviously we're taking your application seriously. You've put your time in, and you're well respected."

"I appreciate that, sir."

"Your résumé shows that you've worked your entire career right here in Haggerston."

"I grew up here," Matt replied.

"What drew you to apply to South Maitland, then?"

"I'm ready for the next challenge," he said. "And the next step isn't always available in your backyard."

"Was it a difficult choice?"

Matt knew what Mr. Bernard was asking—was he going to regret moving across the state and leaving his hometown, his family and his memories behind. The truth was, he wasn't just willing to go; he needed to go. There were things that he needed to escape, and this job in South Maitland was going to be his salvation.

"Not at all." Matt shook his head and gave an easy smile. "I'm ready to move on."

Mr. Bernard smiled. "Glad to hear it, son. So tell me what makes you the right man for the job."

Matt exhaled slowly, then shrugged. "I've been working toward this step for the last five years. I've been working on my certifications and my management degree for longer than that. This has been my career goal all along. I love what I do. It's not a job, it's my life, and I think that matters."

"And the move across state doesn't pose any complications for you?"

"None." Matt pushed back his chair. "What strengths are most important to you in this hiring process?" It was time to ask a few questions of his own.

"Leadership, flexibility, integrity—" Mr. Bernard nodded slowly. "We also want to step up the community connections with the fire department. The last fire chief, who is retiring, didn't work directly with school or community groups very often, and we'd like to find someone who can provide that personal connection."

Matt had suspected as much, and he felt a surge of reassurance that he'd met Rachel when he had. God had a way of sorting out the details, and he sent up a silent prayer of thanks. If they needed someone who could work with school groups, then he'd just have to buff up his skills—pronto.

"Are you hungry, Mr. Bernard?" he asked suddenly.

"Well, I—" The older man cleared his throat and smiled. "I could think about lunch."

"My treat. There's a diner down the street and we could continue this over the best burger in Montana. Let's call it a working lunch."

"Sounds good to me." The older man smiled and patted his belly. "It's getting to be that time, isn't it?"

Matt rose to his feet and came around the desk to meet him. As Matt opened the door, Rachel's voice filtered from down the hallway as she talked with her son in the reception area.

"Thank you so much for showing us around, Firefighter Johnson," she was saying. "It was nice of you to take the time."

Matt led his guest down the hall toward the door. Rachel and Chris stood with Firefighter Johnson, saying their goodbyes. As he reached the reception desk, Matt gave Chris a friendly grin.

"Hi," Christopher said quietly, and Rachel's gaze flew back in his direction.

"Hi, buddy," Matt said. "Did you like the tour?"

The boy shrugged.

"We did," Rachel answered for him. "Thanks. Come on, Chris. We'd better get going."

They all stepped outside together into the warm July sunlight, and Matt glanced in the direction of his crew, who were parking the fire truck in the middle of the sunny drive, ready to go through the daily inspection checklist. Mr. Bernard angled his steps in the direction of the truck, but Matt hung back. Rachel tugged the elastic out of her hair, and her dark waves swung down around her shoulders. The effect was drastic, her dark eyes framed with raven hair, and her pale complexion seeming even milkier with the contrast. She gave Matt a polite nod.

"Mrs. Carter—"

"Call me Rachel."

"Rachel." He smiled. "Is there anything you need to help you settle in?"

"No, no, that's not why I'm here." Her smile evaporated. "I'm fine. It's all under control. We're just about settled."

"Good." He cleared his throat. "Look, you mentioned helping out a bit around here—"

"Absolutely."

"Considering that you're a teacher—" he glanced down at Chris "—and a mom, you're probably my resident expert on kids. I'm not good with school groups, and I'd really like to buff up my skills. Do you think you could help me out?"

"I'd love to." A smile broke over her face, and he was momentarily taken aback by the transformation. She was stunning.

"I've got your number." He patted his front pocket. "Do you mind if I use it?"

"Not at all." Her dark eyes sparkled.

I love that smile. Again, not the most appropriate thought at a time like this, and Mr. Bernard was headed back in their direction.

"I've got to get going," he said, nodding in Mr. Bernard's direction. "But I'll give you a call."

"No problem. I'll see you later." She raised her dark eyes to meet his, then turned her attention to her son. Matt raised a hand in a wave as Rachel and Christopher walked down the pavement toward a white hatchback sedan that had seen better days. Chris looked back at him once with an unreadable expression and Matt couldn't help feeling that he'd unwittingly let the boy down. He wasn't the hero that Chris was looking for.

He wasn't the hero anyone else had been looking for, either, and the biggest reminder of that hard fact was Broxton Park Elementary School.

The school was opening again, teachers were being hired and life was going to continue. He understood that it had to, but something inside him just couldn't move on with everyone else. That fire had done more than gut a school; it had taken the life of a little girl named Natalie Martin—a little girl he'd done his utmost to rescue. He couldn't forget that soot-streaked face, so ashen and pale, or the ragged sobs of her parents, who stood on the sidewalk outside the flaming building clinging to each other.

Haggerston would never forget Natalie, but it would move on. Matt would never forget Natalie, either, but he wouldn't be able to move on here. There were too many memories around every corner, and he knew the answer—South Maitland.

Sometimes God provided healing, and this time, Matt was pretty sure God was providing escape. Maybe healing could happen with some distance.

Rachel dropped the rag back into the sudsy bucket and leaned back on her heels. Renting Grandma's old house from her aunt had seemed like the perfect solution when she moved back to Haggerston, but she hadn't factored in the sheer amount of elbow grease it would take to clean the place up. Rachel looked into the freshly wiped kitchen cupboard and nodded in satisfaction. The 1950s farmhouse kitchen still sported the same teal paint from its early days when her grandmother had set up her own home as a newly married woman. The whitewashed walls, now less than white, contrasted with the teal cupboards, and a big, old-fashioned sink dominated the counter space. A Formica table of the same faded teal held buckets and cleaning products, but under it all, Rachel recognized that familiar, sunny kitchen.

"I always did love Grandma's house," she said.

Her aunt Louise, perched on a chair to reach the inside of the upper shelves, emerged from the depths of a cupboard and eyed her over her glasses. Short, graying hair curled around her face, and her cheeks glowed with the combination of heat and exertion.

"Why didn't you move back earlier?" Louise pushed her glasses up on her face with one arm, keeping her rubber-gloved hands free. "This house has been empty this whole time, you know."

"I know." Rachel rose to her feet. "But when Ed died, I didn't want to leave our home. It felt like leaving him behind."

If she had to be brutally honest with herself, she was pretty angry with Ed, too, for having left *her* behind. They were supposed to grow old together. Ed's dying wasn't part of the deal.

Her aunt nodded. "This is good for Christopher, though. He needs family."

Rachel glanced upward, toward the boy's bedroom on the second floor. Overhead, the odd thump echoed down through the ceiling from his unpacking efforts.

"I hope so," she said softly.

"*You* need family." Aunt Louise shot her a pointed look.

Rachel grinned. "I know. And here we are."

Louise gave a curt nod and disappeared back into the cupboard once more. Rachel stood motionless, her mind moving over the memories of childhood summers. Hot apple pie, sweet iced tea, old family stories, visits to the graveyard, where she used to read the inscriptions on her great-grandparents' gravestones, feeling connected to the generations who came before her... Haggerston had been a warm, safe place for Rachel, and she hoped that somehow her own pleasant memories would morph into something more tangible for her son. Was it even possible to channel her happy childhood memories into his boyhood years?

A knock from the front door echoed through the empty house, and Rachel peeled off her rubber gloves and dropped them onto the side of the bucket, then went to answer the door. She paused at the foot of the stairs, just able to make out her son's legs as he scampered down the upstairs hallway. She smiled to herself and pulled open the front door.

Matt Bailey stood on the porch, his navy blue uniform shirt open at the neck and the summer breeze ruffling his sun-bleached hair. He dropped his gaze, then lifted his eyes to meet hers tentatively.

"Hi," he said.

"Hello." A thump overhead drew both of their attention, and she chuckled. "Chris is unpacking up there."

"Sounds like he's enjoying himself." He glanced upward, in the direction of the thumps. "Sorry to just stop in on you like this. I saw your car, so I figured you'd be here."

Rachel looked past his broad shoulders to her white hatchback, rusting around the wheel wells and badly in need of a wash. "You found me. I'm just renting right now, but this is actually my grandmother's old house, so—"

From the kitchen, Louise called, "I told you a thousand times, Rachel, I'm not accepting a penny from you!"

Rachel laughed and shook her head. "That's Aunt Louise. She has ears like a cat. Be warned."

Matt's eyes crinkled in a warm smile. "Sounds like you're in good hands." The smile faltered, and he met her gaze frankly. "I wanted to apologize about today."

"Oh, it's no matter." Rachel batted her hand through the air.

"No, it is." He cleared his throat. "I wasn't expecting to meet Chris today, and I wasn't at my best. Is he okay?"

Rachel's mind went to the silent drive home she and Christopher had shared—a quiet boy fiddling with a paper plane in the back of the car, his usual noisy exuberance dampened. She wasn't about to make that Matt's problem, though. "He'll be all right."

"Okay. Good." Matt cleared his throat, and his gaze softened. "It was nice to meet you. Both of you."

Inside the house, the phone rang, and Louise picked it up with a singsong "Hello?" Rachel angled her head toward the door and stepped outside. Matt followed. One side of the porch was overgrown with a lilac bush, the clustered blossoms breathing out fragrance, and the other side basked in the shade of a mature oak tree. She let her gaze wander over the yard, a little overgrown and in need of mowing, and then back to her tall guest. Matt's uniform shirt was wrinkled up the back, and his chin glistened with stubble in the late-afternoon sunlight.

"I should apologize, too," she confessed. "I didn't mean to come on so strongly back at the firehouse. I get something into my head, and I just go full steam ahead. I guess I'd hoped—" She brushed some errant wisps of hair away from her forehead. "I don't even know what I hoped. I'm sorry about that."

"No, it's okay. It sounds pretty complicated, actually."

"It is." She pushed her fingers into her snug jeans pockets. "But that isn't your problem. I'll take care of it."

"Yeah, of course." He nodded curtly and took a step back, his eyes moving over the wooden porch, paint flaking away from the sagging boards. "Did you know that I knew your grandmother? I don't know why you and I never met."

"Did you? I didn't realize that. I used to come to visit in the summers for a couple of weeks, but never for terribly long."

"That would explain why I don't remember you." He shot her a boyish grin, and for a moment she thought he might be flirting, but then he looked away. "Your grandmother was a nice lady. She used to bring us homemade cookies at the firehouse."

"That sounds like Grandma." Rachel chuckled. "She fed absolutely everyone."

She also had a soft spot for firefighters, something that Ed had always appreciated.

"No complaints here." Matt crossed his muscular arms over his chest. "She made the best macaroons in town. That included my own grandmother's macaroons."

"That's some high praise, then." Rachel smiled. "This seems like a great place for a kid to grow up."

"The best." Something flickered deep in his eyes at those words, but before she could think more of it, a window scraped open on the second floor over their heads, and Christopher's voice hollered down, "Mom!"

Rachel trotted down the steps to look up at her son's smiling face.

"Are you exploring up there?" Rachel asked with a laugh.

"Yeah, I found old hats."

"That's fun."

"And a really big spider."

Rachel shuddered. "Don't touch it."

"I can't reach it," Chris replied, which meant that he'd

have caught it already if it had been lower to the floor. She could be thankful for small mercies.

"Mr. Bailey came by to say hello," she said, and Matt ambled up next to her, his warm arm emanating heat against her slender shoulder.

"Hi." Chris's tone turned shyer.

"I was hoping I could take you and Chris out for dinner tonight," Matt said, his gaze moving from Rachel to Chris and back again. "If you aren't busy, that is."

"Actually Aunt Louise is cooking for us," she replied. "It would have been nice, though."

"How about tomorrow evening?" he asked.

Rachel nodded with a smile. "That would work. Thanks. I'm sure Chris would like the chance to talk to you a bit more."

"I don't know what to say to Chris, but I'll do my best," he confessed, his tone dropping low enough for her ears alone.

Rachel shrugged. "Don't worry too much. You're already a hero in his eyes."

A smile slid across his rugged features and he looked up at the boy in the open window. "See you later, Chris. I'm glad I got to meet you."

Chris wordlessly raised his hand in a wave, and Matt turned back to Rachel.

"What time should I pick you up tomorrow?"

Rachel paused, uncertainty flickering deep inside her. This felt too familiar already, too intimate, and dating was the furthest from her intentions. She had a little boy who needed some stability right now, and this handsome firefighter didn't exactly fit into her plans for some peace and quiet. Besides, she'd been married to a firefighter once already, and loving him as she had, she'd promised herself that she'd never marry another one. She didn't think she could handle losing another man she loved to the perils of the job.

"Why don't we meet you at the restaurant?" she countered.

He nodded. "Sure. Does Chris like pizza?"

"Yes!" Chris hollered from the window above, and Rachel chuckled.

"You have your answer there."

"Great. Alphonzo's Pizza is on the corner of Main Street, right across from the drugstore. Do you know the place I mean?"

Rachel held up her phone. "I'll find it with my GPS. How does six o'clock sound?"

"Perfect. See you then." He shot her a grin, then ambled back toward his truck. With his hand on the door handle, he turned back and called up to the second-story window, "Chris, they've got ice cream, too. Just saying."

Rachel smothered a laugh and watched as Matt hopped up into the cab of the white pickup, a red fire-department seal emblazoned across the side. The vehicle roared to life and he pulled away from the curb. As she turned back toward the house, Rachel stopped short when she saw her aunt standing in the doorway.

"You startled me." She chuckled. "I didn't know you were there."

"I know." Louise raised an eyebrow teasingly and turned back into the house. "Handsome young fellow, isn't he?"

"He's a firefighter, Auntie. It's not going to happen."

"I always liked firefighters… So did Grandma," Louise pointed out with exaggerated casualness.

Rachel rolled her eyes and followed her aunt indoors.

"I know, I know…"

And so it starts, she thought wryly. If there was one thing she was sure of, it was that a town filled with aunts, uncles and distant cousins would never sit idly by and leave her business alone. That was too much to ask.

Chapter Two

As Matt pulled away, he glanced back at the old house. It needed paint—and a lot more—to look decent again, but he could already see the spark of a family in the old place. Stacks of boxes were visible in the windows, and a pile of cardboard sat outside the garage. If memory served, the big oak tree in the front yard used to have a tire swing that all the neighborhood kids made use of, and he idly wondered if Rachel would put up another one for Chris. Maybe he was already too old for a tire swing. Matt wasn't exactly in the know when it came to kids. He was the kind of relative who gave his cousins' kids cash when he saw them because he could never quite remember their birthdays and wanted to make sure he covered his bases.

Matt glanced at the old houses on either side of the street, flower gardens in bloom. A few of the homes sported American flags, rippling proudly in the summer wind, and he sighed. If he got this job, he had to admit, he would miss Haggerston.

His cell phone rang, and he glanced down at the number as he slowed to a stop at an intersection. It was his brother. Matt put the phone on speaker, tossed it onto the seat beside him and eased the vehicle forward again.

"Hi, Craig," he said.

"Hey, how did that interview go?" his brother asked.

"Really good. They're taking me seriously."

"Fantastic."

"But that wasn't the most interesting part of my day," he admitted.

"Oh, yeah?" Craig pried.

"Do you remember that time a few years ago when a baby was dropped off on the doorstep of the firehouse?"

"I think so."

"Well, he's back."

"The baby?"

"Yeah." Matt chuckled. "Well, he's about seven now. His adoptive mother moved into town, and they stopped by the firehouse to say hi. I guess she wanted to show him where he was found."

"How's the kid doing?"

"Okay." He paused. "Maybe not so well. His mom says that her husband died a few years ago, and the kid only recently found out that he's adopted, so that's been pretty hard on him."

"Ouch. I'll bet."

"So I stopped by their place to—" Matt cringed. This still sounded very much like a date. "I asked them out to dinner."

"Is that a good idea? They just moved here, and you're planning to move on."

"Not like that," Matt grumbled. "I know how it sounds. I didn't really get much of a chance to talk to Chris, and I wanted to chat with him a bit. His mother seems to think it will help."

He signaled at the next stop sign and took a left toward the main road. The houses in this direction were smaller and the yards not as well tended. He knew several of the people on this street, however. Living his entire life in one town had that effect.

"And what about the mother?" his brother pressed.

"What about her?" Matt dodged.

"Still single?"

"Yes, still single," he replied. "And before you ask, yes, she's pretty."

"Aha."

"Oh, cut it out." Matt laughed and slowed for another corner. "She's the widow of a firefighter from Billings, so I feel like I owe her something. It's not romantic, I swear."

There was a muffled voice in the background, and then his brother came back. "Gloria's inviting you to our place for dinner," Craig said. "Are you interested? I could pop another steak on the barbecue."

The thought of a barbecue steak made Matt's stomach rumble, and he chuckled. "Twist my arm, man. I'm on my way. Can I pick up anything?"

"No, we're ready to go. Just get down here, because I'm hungry."

"Okay, I'm ten minutes away."

Matt hung up and smiled ruefully. He'd miss his brother and his wife, too, if he moved out of town. Craig and Gloria had him over for dinner about as often as he'd let them. He begged off more often than not, preferring to give them time to themselves, being newlyweds and all.

He eased forward again and glanced toward the squat elementary school. Brand-new play equipment sprawled on one side of the building, a green field on the other side. A sign in front of the building announced student registration days and encouraged everyone to "Find adventure in reading this summer." The scars from the fire were cleaned away, and this September, Broxton Park Elementary would reopen for the first time since that tragic day.

He had no idea what anyone else saw when they looked at that building, but in his mind's eye he still saw the billowing smoke pouring out of broken windows. He still heard the frightened screams of children, the wail of sirens and the desperate, clinging questions of the parents standing in shocked groups on the sidewalk.

He'd fought fires for most of his adult life, and the very thought of a blazing inferno only got his adrenaline pumping and made him twitch to jump into his boots. This school represented more than a fire, though. It represented his own personal failure and the death of a child.

Matt heaved a sigh as he passed the building and crossed another intersection. This school always affected him the same way. His stomach curdled and sweat sprang out on his palms. He knew he was a good firefighter. He knew he'd followed all the protocol possible in that fire, and he knew that he wasn't liable or at fault, but somehow that didn't change a thing.

Matt willed his pounding heart to quiet, and he signaled for another turn onto his brother's street.

He'd eat steak. He'd compliment his sister-in-law's pasta salad, and he'd jokingly rebuff all of Gloria's attempts to set him up and get him married. It was Wednesday night, and he knew the drill.

Lord, he prayed silently, *I need this job.*

* * *

The next evening, the aroma of pizza drifted down Main Street, mingling with the scent of the hanging planters that hung from lampposts, dripping a lazy rhythm from a recent watering. Alphonzo's Pizza crouched on one corner, nestled up against Duggar Jewelers. Golden sunlight bathed the street, contrasting with the long shadows. Six o'clock constituted dinnertime in Haggerston, and the streets were deserted, save for the rumble of the odd pickup truck. Almost all of the local businesses had closed up shop for the evening, with the exception of Alphonzo's Pizza.

Inside the restaurant, Rachel and Chris sat at a table in the far corner, listening to the distant din of the kitchen. A paper menu in the center of the table showed the meal options—everything from pizza to chop suey—and Chris fiddled with the corner, a bored look on his face.

"Hi, hon," a young waitress crooned, pulling a pad of paper from her pocket. "What can I get you to start?"

"Could we get my son a pop?" she asked. "What kind, sweetie?"

"Orange, please."

"Sure thing." The waitress jotted it down. "And for you?"

"Actually we're waiting for someone, so maybe I'll wait until he arrives."

As if on cue, the bell above the door tinkled and Matt stepped inside, pulling off his sunglasses. He was out of uniform today, wearing a pair of jeans and a blue polo shirt that strained slightly around his biceps. He glanced around the restaurant, his steely gaze falling on them.

"Oh, here he is," Rachel said and smiled up at Matt as he approached the table. He slid into the chair opposite

Rachel, and while they ordered soft drinks and a pepperoni pizza, she found herself studying his face. A pale scar cut past one eyebrow, a detail she hadn't noticed earlier. He seemed gentler out of uniform, more accessible, less official. His sun-bleached hair had a touch of premature gray working through the front, and as he leaned his elbows on the tabletop, the scent of aftershave lingered.

"So, how are you liking Haggerston?" Matt asked after the waitress left the table.

"I've always loved this town," she said. "I wanted to move here years ago."

"Why didn't you?"

"My husband was with the Billings Fire Department, and he was happy there. He was climbing." She shrugged. "What can you do?"

He nodded. "It's hard to move on once your life is rooted somewhere else. I get that."

"This is the perfect tiny town. The flowers on the street corners, the shops where everyone knows each other—"

"You like the idea of everyone knowing you?" he asked with a wry smile.

"Maybe?" She laughed softly. "In some ways it's comforting, but I'm sure there is a flip side to the coin. What about you? How long have you lived here?"

"I grew up here, so if I'm not related to someone, I probably know them somehow." He grinned. "Our waitress babysits my cousin's kids."

"Seriously?" Rachel looked back at the young woman taking another table's order. "It's a small world."

"It's a small town," he corrected with a low laugh.

"Did you know my mom, Mr. Bailey?" Chris locked

his gaze on the firefighter's face, all the intensity of his seven years focused on the man across the table from him, and Rachel shifted uncomfortably. She knew that her son had questions, and it looked as though he was ready to ask a few of them.

"I just met her the other day, with you," Matt replied, his gaze flickering toward Rachel.

"No, I mean my other mom," he pressed. "The one who left me at the firehouse. Did you know her?"

Rachel's stomach dropped. He'd been asking about his birth mother lately, and she somehow hoped that he would never need to know more about the woman than she'd already told him and that she could be enough. She wasn't, though, and she didn't have the answers, either. All she wanted right now was to be able to fill in the gaps for him, to help soothe his unease and confusion.

"Uh…" Matt looked up at Rachel uncertainly, then back to the boy's earnest gaze. "I never did find out who she was, buddy. I'm sorry."

"It's okay." Chris shrugged. "I just wondered."

"You have a really good mom right here," Matt said. "She loves you a whole lot."

"Yeah, I love her, too." Chris leaned back in his chair, but his eyes were still clouded.

The food arrived. A large pepperoni pizza oozing melted cheese and still sizzling from the oven was deposited in the center of the table. After everyone was served and Chris took a big bite of pizza, Rachel sucked in a deep breath.

"I know that Chris wants to hear about how he was found," she said. Chris's attention snapped up.

"Sure." Matt cleared his throat. "Do you know anything about that night, Chris?"

"A little bit," the boy replied past a cheek full of food.

"I was working the night shift, and I was watching a training video. Someone buzzed downstairs—a woman—asking me to come down. I didn't know what to expect, so I went on down."

"Was that my mom?" Chris asked after swallowing.

Every time Chris referred to his birth mother as "his mom," it stung just a little. Rachel had imagined these conversations countless times over the years, but she'd never fully appreciated how difficult it was for a mother to share her child. She should have been discussing this with him long ago, and if she hadn't been so crushed by Ed's death, she would have.

"I'm assuming so," Matt said with a nod. "When I got down there, she was gone, and you were there. In a box."

"Was I small?"

"You were pretty tiny, buddy."

"Did I cry?"

"A little bit. You were hungry."

"So you fed me?"

"We had some bottles and formula on hand in case of emergency, and I guess you counted as an emergency. So I sat in a big armchair, and I fed you your bottle. You slurped that thing back like nobody's business, and then you settled in for a nice nap."

"How long did you hold him for?" Rachel asked softly.

"It took about three hours for Social Services to arrive. So I just sat there and held him. He was cold." He glanced at Rachel uneasily, and she suspected there was more to the story, details he couldn't share in front of Chris.

"What's that services thing?" Chris asked.

"Social Services take care of people when they need help. They came to get you, and they found you a good home where you would be safe and loved. That's how your mom and dad got you."

"We got a call that night." Rachel continued the story. "They said a baby needed a safe home, and they asked if we'd take care of you. We drove down and picked you up, and I knew the moment I saw you that I'd never let you go."

"But what about my mom?" Chris asked, and Rachel pushed back the sting.

"I don't know, Chris," she said quietly. "Your birth mother left you at the fire station, and no one ever found out who she was. But I know that she wanted you to be safe. She brought you to the one place she could be sure that someone would take care of you."

Chris put his attention back into his pizza, and when Rachel glanced back in Matt's direction, she found his warm gaze enveloping her. He reached across the table and took her hand in his broad, warm grasp, giving her a squeeze. He released her fingers almost as quickly as he'd taken them, but she was grateful for the gesture.

"Chris, I saw some video games over there in the corner," Matt said. He leaned back in his seat and fished around in his pocket, his hand emerging with a fistful of quarters. "Do you want to try them?"

"Can I, Mom?" Chris turned bright, exuberant eyes onto Rachel, the previous heaviness apparently forgotten.

She smiled and nodded. "Sure, sweetie. Have fun."

Chris accepted the quarters into his cupped palms and headed off toward the video games. They looked almost antique—Pac-Man, some racing games and a claw that dipped into a vat of dusty plush toys. He looked so grown up, standing there with his quarters, and yet so small, all at once.

This move to Haggerston was supposed to give Chris the stability he craved, yet even here, she felt his struggle. He couldn't put words to it—he was too young to even try. She knew what was in his heart, though.

Who did he belong to?

And her heart replied with every beat, *You belong to me.*

Matt leaned his elbows on the table and stabbed at some ice cubes in his glass with a straw. Rachel looked toward her son, and when her gaze flickered back in his direction, color rose in her cheeks. She was gorgeous— and every time emotion sparkled in those dark eyes, he found his thoughts sliding into dangerous territory.

"He's growing up so fast," she said.

Matt nodded. "I can only imagine."

"He's been asking about his birth mother a lot lately." She breathed a sigh. "This isn't easy."

"She did what was best for him," he said. "I didn't want to say this in front of Chris, but he was in rough shape when I found him. He was in a wet cardboard box. His sleeper was soaked, his diaper was dirty and his bottle was rancid. He shivered in my arms for a full hour, and he drank bottle after bottle. I doubt he was getting enough milk before he was dropped off at the firehouse. He was so desperate for human touch that once he figured I'd protect him, he wouldn't let anyone else touch him."

She froze at those words, and he immediately regretted them. "I'm sorry. That was probably too blunt."

"No, no…" She shook her head, blinking back the tears that sprang to her eyes. "I was told about his condition by the authorities, but hearing it from you—" She swallowed, not finishing the thought.

Idiot, he chastised himself. *She didn't need to hear it like that.*

"She brought him to the right place," he said, his voice low. "And he went to the right home."

Her dark gaze met his, and he was struck by those liquid eyes. Long lashes brushed her cheekbones with each blink, and a soft pink tinged her cheeks. She gave a weak shrug.

"I'd do anything for him. He's really struggling."

"You're a good mom," he replied. "He'll be okay."

She nodded and sucked in a deep breath. "I think Haggerston is just what Chris needs. I keep saying that, but I really do believe it. Sometimes a fresh start is just the ticket."

Her words struck on the deepest longing inside him, too. She wanted to start over here in Haggerston, and he wanted to start over as far from this town as he could get, but they both wanted the same thing. They wanted to leave behind the old barbs and wounds and start over again—get another kick at the can without the pain that weighed them down. Was it even possible? He sure hoped so, because it was his last hope.

"Couldn't agree more." He reached for another slice of pizza.

"I was wondering about something." She paused, a frown creasing her brow. "When they hired me at Broxton Park Elementary, they mentioned that it had a fire a few years ago."

Matt nodded. "A big one."

"That's scary. Were you there for it?"

"Yeah." *There for it* was an understatement. He returned to that dreadful morning in his dreams, where he endlessly searched with his gloved hands, through the murky darkness. He pushed back the memories.

"That had to be terrifying for everyone. How do you do that?" Her thoughtful gaze moved over his face.

"It's my job."

"I know, but…" She paused, her intent eyes fixed on him. "Aren't you scared in situations like that?"

"I'm well trained." The training was intense. A firefighter learned to react before he felt, to obey an order and question it later. Like in the military, a quick response to command was the secret to success, and for a firefighter, success meant getting everyone out alive.

"I understand the training because my husband went through it, but I never could quite understand how someone could subvert every instinct in his body telling him to get out of there. That's just simple self-preservation."

She was right about that, but it was something they didn't talk about. Being afraid was part of the job, but if they talked about it and fed it, then they were useless in the face of an emergency. Firefighters didn't talk about fear; they talked about preparation.

"I'm suited up, I've got a buddy system and I'm much better prepared for that heat than the victims are. I'm pretty much just focused on finding people and getting them out."

"You must have a lot of stories."

Matt chuckled. "Most of the job is paperwork. We do prefire inspections, public education, that sort of thing. I do a lot of reports. Like this restaurant, for example."

He glanced around them, quickly estimating the risks

in the room. Rachel looked around the dining room, following his gaze.

"There are two exits—the door I came in, and a door out the back." He hooked a thumb toward the front door. "These tables would be like an obstacle course, especially through the smoke. The kitchen is worse, but those prefire safety inspections give us a lay of the land, so to speak. We want to know a building's layout before we have to stampede in there in full gear. We have a job, and we know what we have to do."

"So you're saying you're too focused to get scared?" she asked.

He chuckled again, amused at her tenacity. She wasn't going to let this go, was she? He shrugged. "We're too well trained to admit to it."

Rachel was silent for a moment. "So, was that the training taking over the first day we met you?"

He raised an eyebrow, considering. "I guess so, yeah. I've learned to lean back on the training when I feel—" He stopped, uncertain of even how to decipher the complicated emotions he felt when seeing Chris again for the first time.

"Scared?" she suggested.

He shrugged. "Scared? Maybe. Nervous. Uncertain. Off balance. Anyway, I either knock down doors or spout statistics. As you found out." He smiled and she laughed softly.

"It makes sense. And thank God for your training—it saves lives."

"Not enough lives," he replied. All the training in the world couldn't bring back Natalie Martin. He'd seen countless school pictures around town of the little girl, clean and brightly smiling. That wasn't the face seared into his memory, however. He would always remember the face smeared with grime, eyes streaming from the smoke and her hair a tangled mess. He's see her ashen cheeks as she lay unconscious in his arms. He couldn't remember what he felt in those exact moments. He felt it later, when he lay in his bed that night after the fire had been extinguished, the day's events playing through his mind. That was when the reality of the situation hit him.

"Amen to that," she said quietly, and his gaze snapped up to meet hers. He'd momentarily forgotten about her husband, and he winced.

"I'm sorry. I forgot about your husband."

She shook her head. "I have to admit, I'm still angry about his death."

"It was pointless," he said.

"Exactly. Pointless. But that's what firefighters do. They put themselves in harm's way in order to save people."

"Did they save lives that day?" he asked. The risk was worth it if lives were saved—that was what kept a firefighter going.

"The truck driver didn't make it out…" She looked away toward her son, playing video games. "They both died that day."

No rescues. Two deaths. His stomach sank.

"When you're in that kind of situation," he said, "your training has to move faster than your emotions do. You let your brain catch up when there's time. Your husband was in the zone. He wouldn't have been afraid, if that helps you at all."

"It does, actually."

He could tell that she hadn't made her peace with everything yet, and he couldn't blame her. It had been a year since Natalie Martin's death, and he still hadn't made his peace with it. She hadn't been the first person to die in a fire, and she wouldn't be the last. They were only people putting it all on the line for other people's families, but somehow this one little girl had gotten past all his defenses.

"Are you a Christian, Matt?"

Matt pulled his mind back from the precipice. "I am."

"Me, too." Rachel's gaze roamed over the restaurant, settling on her son across the room. "Does it help?"

"I suppose my faith is a part of everything I do," he said quietly. "But even faith doesn't answer every question, does it?"

"I suppose not." She pushed her glossy waves away from her face. "You've been through a lot, haven't you?"

"There are people who have gone through far worse than I ever have."

An image of Natalie's grief-stricken parents arose in his mind. They'd been in shock, their faces white, their eyes begging him to take it all away as if that fire-retardant suit gave him supernatural power. But he couldn't. Natalie was part of the reason why he needed to learn about children. Natalie had run from him when he came to rescue her…and he never wanted that to happen again.

"Look," Matt said, tearing his mind away from those old wounds. "Do you think you could give me some of those tips for working with kids?"

"Now?" She took a sip of her pop.

"How about tomorrow? If that isn't too soon."

"I'd be happy to." She nodded. "I can bring by a few resources, if I find the right box tonight. What time works for you?"

"How about two at my office?"

She smiled. "Sure."

Chris came dashing back across the room, zigzagging around tables. He arrived at their table, out of breath and with a grin on his face.

"I won something!" He held up a small stuffed rabbit in a victorious display. As the boy exuberantly showed his mother his hard-won prize, Matt fell gratefully silent. He'd done enough talking, more than he'd ever intended. He took a deep breath, mentally steeling himself.

"It's really hard to get one," Chris was explaining. "It came down like this—" He used his hand to mime the game. "And then it went like this…"

Rachel's gaze flickered in Matt's direction and her gentle eyes crinkled into a smile. Before he could catch himself, he felt his own return grin tickling the corners of his lips. He picked up the dessert menu, a sundae awash in chocolate sauce and crowned with fluffy whipped cream emblazoned across the top.

"Let's order that ice cream. What do you say?"

Chapter Three

The next afternoon, Rachel leaned back in the chair across from Matt's desk. The air-conditioning felt good after a morning of unpacking in the overheated house. Most people had personal effects in their work space, but Matt didn't seem to have much. No pictures of pets or family, no crayon artwork, no tacky gag gifts. This space shone clean and efficient. Her desk at school was always covered with "I love my teacher" gifts and eraser collections. The kids liked to come look at her desk, and she'd use the erasers as rewards for good behavior through the year. Perhaps it was her background in elementary education, but this amount of order seemed sad. Everyone needed a little love, and love, most often, came in the form of some organized chaos.

Then again, that might be the mother in her, too.

Matt leaned forward, catching her eye as her gaze swung back to where the big firefighter sat across from her in his desk.

"And this will work?" he asked.

"Teaching is less of a science and more of an art," she admitted, pulling her mind back to her purpose in this pristine space. "When you have the same class every day, you learn which children get distracted more easily and which catch on more quickly. But when you have a different group of children every day, it's more challenging."

She'd been giving him a quick introduction to elementary-aged teaching, and he'd taken a few notes and questioned her for the past half hour. He seemed serious about this, which impressed her. Not many people worked so hard to improve their weak areas.

"So you're saying to keep them engaged individually, and that will encourage them to pay attention."

"Exactly." She nodded. "If you call on kids randomly to ask them questions, ask their opinion or just use them in an example, the kids will want to listen because they might get your attention next. There will always be a few who distract the class, but at least you'll have most of their attention."

"So this is pretty much on-the-fly decision making."

"Pretty much," she agreed. "It takes a little practice, but it works."

"What about a problem kid?" he asked.

"A ringleader of sorts?"

"Exactly. How do you deal with one causing trouble?"

"Engage him. You don't have time to discipline or anything like that. You're trying to give them information in a way that they'll remember it. That's all. You won't be seeing these kids again, so don't make it into a power struggle. You want to get the ringleader's attention and ask him for his opinion about something. Don't make it into a punishment. Ask him honestly. You'll have the entire class's attention, including your ringleader. That's priceless."

"Great," he said, jotting something down on paper.

"And then there is always The Look. Most of the time a warning is better than a punishment. It takes a bit of practice, but it's useful."

"Let's see it."

Rachel shot Matt her most teacherly look of warning. He froze, eyes locked on her, and his lips slightly parted.

"Yikes." He rose to his feet and chuckled. "Seriously, that's some potent stuff there. Be careful where you point that. I'm not sure what for, but I feel mildly guilty now... and I have this urge to raise my hand before I speak."

"Oh, good, I haven't lost it," she joked.

"I'm not even sure I could reproduce that," he confessed. He shot her a serious and mildly quizzical look. "That's all I've got. That's the look I give my firefighters under me when they do something really dumb. But yours—that's a thing of art."

"Yeah, it's not the same," she agreed with a wry smile. "Maybe it's a mom thing."

Matt shot her a grin, then glanced at his watch. "I'm officially done here for the day. Do you have anywhere you need to be?"

"I promised myself I'd go for a walk this afternoon and get some exercise," she replied, pushing herself to her feet. "That's about it."

"Care for some company?" His clear gaze met hers and a smile turned up the corners of his lips.

Part of her knew she should decline his tempting offer, but somehow she couldn't bring herself to utter the words. "Sure."

She glanced around the office once more in an attempt to distract herself. He turned off his computer and dropped a few papers into a filing cabinet, his muscular arms flexing as he stretched to reach a file folder.

"Matt, you have the most sterile office I've ever seen," she said.

"Do I?" He looked around. "What's wrong with it?"

"I can't tell anything about you by looking at this space. There are no pictures…nothing."

"The way I like it." He shot her a teasing grin.

"Why?"

He didn't answer as they headed down the hallway and into the reception area. The receptionist looked up with a tired smile, but her gaze flickered in Rachel's direction with interest.

"Good night, Joyce," Matt said over his shoulder.

"Good night," she replied, then shot Rachel a sugary smile. "You take care of him, now."

Rachel wasn't sure how to answer that and opted for silence. As they exited the door into the summer sunlight, she glanced up at Matt questioningly.

"And that is exactly why I keep things private." He chuckled. "In a place this size, everyone's curious."

A cool breeze whisked by, lifting her dark hair over her face. She pulled her fingers through her hair, holding it back as she glanced up at him.

"A few photos around the office might put the rumors to rest," she suggested.

"Photos of what?" He shrugged. "My last vacation that I took alone? A picture of me taken by another tourist? No, that's just depressing."

"Don't you have a cat or a dog?"

He shook his head. "Sorry."

"Maybe a picture of your mom, then." She shot him a grin.

"Absolutely not." Matt laughed. "That's how a guy gets to be known as a mama's boy."

"Is that so terrible?" she joked.

"That's coming from a mother," he replied with a chuckle. "I love my mom, and she knows it. When I get married, I'll put my wife's picture on my desk. Happy?"

"It'll have to do."

"Trust me, the mystery is better than the reality."

"And what's the reality?"

"A whole lot of work and not much of a social life." His eyes crinkled up into a smile. "I might need to get a dog so people stop feeling sorry for me."

The sun peeked from behind a cloud, then disappeared again. Clouds were moving in, the air cooling. The hum of a lawn mower floated over the breeze, bringing along with it the scent of freshly cut grass. The fire station was on the corner of a well-established residential area, and they angled their steps down a tree-lined street, Matt with his hands in his pockets and Rachel sauntering beside him. The houses on either side of them were small bungalows, and the trees that stretched over the road were mature. Matt glanced in her direction.

"Thanks for all your help today. I owe you one."

"No, don't worry about it," she replied with a shake of her head. "I feel a little bad for the rumors your receptionist is about to start…"

He grinned. "It's inevitable."

"But she's new, right?" she asked. "Maybe she'll be properly in awe of you and restrain herself."

"I doubt it." He laughed. "She might be new to the firehouse, but she's also the church pianist. The familiarity is already there."

"You really can't win, can you?" she teased.

A cooler breeze enveloped her in a chilly embrace. Clouds rolled in more quickly now, a dark, smudgy blanket moving over the town, carrying with it the electric scent of promised rain.

"With all the people you know around town," she began, "why did you ask me to help you? I'm sure you know teachers and day-care providers, and—"

He looked down at her, regret swimming in his clear eyes. "I've applied for a job across the state," he said. "It's not definite, so I need to be discreet. Anyone else would pass the word in a heartbeat."

She attempted to cover her surprise by looking down. So he wasn't planning on sticking around Haggerston anyway. That would be a good thing to keep in mind when Chris got to know him.

"Oh..." She cleared her throat.

"I hope that isn't crass." He grimaced. "I'm not suggesting that you have no friends—"

She attempted to smile casually. "No, I get it. It's no problem. I'll keep that little detail to myself." It wasn't her place to pass around rumors, and she wasn't naive about the speed of gossip in a place this size.

"Thanks. I appreciate it."

So he was heading out of town, if all went according to plan. It was good to know, and it helped. Matt Bailey was charming and handsome, and it certainly gave her more willpower to know that he wasn't going to stick around—not that she actually needed any more excuses to stay out of a relationship. Chris had gone through enough changes lately, and she doubted he could handle it if his mom started dating. Besides, a firefighter's life held no mystery for her. She knew all about the long hours, the middle-of-the-night calls to fill in for someone who was sick, the constant danger and the wear and tear on a marriage. That uniform might be appealing, but the lifestyle was not.

As if on cue, thunder rumbled overhead and Rachel squinted up at the ever-darkening clouds.

"It's going to rain," Matt said. "Come on."

"Shouldn't we head back?" she asked, quickening her pace to keep up with his long stride.

"This is closer," he replied. "I live just down Oak Street."

Rachel ducked her head against the first mist of rain and she grimaced inwardly. Rain and moisture were going to do a number on her straightened hair.

I'm the mother of a first grader, still worrying about my hair blowout.

A clap of thunder boomed overhead, and with it came a deluge of rain, pounding down onto them like a thousand tiny fists. Matt scooped up her hand in his and broke into a jog, tugging her along, pulling her closer against his broad, muscular shoulder.

"We're going to be drenched!" Rachel laughed breathlessly. Water dripped down her face, slicking her fuchsia T-shirt against her skin. Matt's hand tightened around hers as they crossed a street, his head ducked against the rain.

"Looks like." He chuckled, the sound warm and deep. "Don't worry. I've got coffee."

As they jumped over a puddle already forming by the curb, Matt pointed to a little house across the next street, a white-trimmed bungalow, blurred by the falling rain.

"Almost there." His voice was low and close to her ear. With another boom of thunder, they made the last dash toward shelter.

* * *

Matt unlocked the front door and they stumbled inside just as another flash of lightning lit up the sky, followed seconds later by a deafening peal of thunder. Their footsteps echoed in the entryway, and he flicked on a light to compensate for the premature darkness of the storm. He normally kept a pretty clean house, but he did a quick glance around to make sure he hadn't left a T-shirt on the sofa or his barbells on the floor from his morning workout that would betray his manly ways. Rachel stepped inside and shivered. Her hair dripped, the previously smooth waves springing up into sodden curls.

She has curly hair.

He wasn't sure why this discovery made him smile, but it did.

Rachel looked down at the puddle she'd made on the floor. Her jeans were dark with rain and goose bumps prickled across her arms.

"I'm making a mess," she said.

"No more than I am," he replied. His uniform clung to his arms and legs, a steady trickle of water meandering down his back. "Tell you what. If it wouldn't be too awkward, let me give you some of my clothes to wear while we toss yours into the dryer."

She contemplated for a moment, then nodded. "I don't see a way around it. I'm drenched."

While Rachel changed behind the locked bathroom door, Matt grabbed a fresh T-shirt and a pair of jeans for himself out of his dresser drawer. He changed quickly, tossing his wet clothes into a hamper on his way out of the bedroom, and headed toward the kitchen.

Matt grabbed the filters and coffee grounds from the cupboard, feeling more cheerful than he had felt in a while. Outside the kitchen window, the rain came down in sheets, trees heaving with the gusts of wind. His patio chairs rattled in the wind and collected pools of water on the seats, and he paused to watch the low, boiling clouds.

It didn't matter where you went in Montana, the sky remained the same. The same summer storms swept over the state, and he couldn't help wondering if South Maitland would be different enough to drown his memories.

"I found your dryer myself. I hope you don't mind."

Matt turned from the coffeemaker to find Rachel in the kitchen doorway, dwarfed in one of his T-shirts and a pair of sweatpants. Soft wisps of hair began to dry around her cheeks and spiraled into silky curls. She held up the pants with one hand and sank into a kitchen chair.

"I've never felt less put together." She laughed.

"All you need is coffee," he replied with a grin. "How do you take it?"

"Cream and sugar."

The coffeemaker sputtered soothingly in the background. Her gaze wandered around the kitchen, sliding over his black stove and dark cupboards and stopping at his fridge.

"Aha," she said, a triumphant smile coming to her lips. "Finally something personal."

She crossed the kitchen and perused the photos that were stuck there with various magnets.

"Who's this?" she asked, pointing at a wedding photo.

"My brother, Craig, and his new wife, Gloria."

He glanced over her shoulder at the familiar photo. Craig was pulling Gloria close against him, and her head was tilting down to his shoulder. They both beamed into the camera. Matt stood next to his brother in an "at ease" stance, and the maid of honor stood in a pinkish-orange dress, her flowers clutched in front of her. Matt remembered the happiness of that afternoon. Craig and Gloria could have gotten married in a mud puddle and it wouldn't have dampened their spirits.

"You make a very dapper best man." She shot him a smile. "It looks like a beautiful wedding."

"He tried to get out of it," he said with a short laugh.

"You're kidding." She cast him a surprised glance.

"The morning of the wedding, he told me he was leaving town. So I did the only thing I could."

"Called the bride?" Rachel asked.

"Duct-taped him to a kitchen chair and talked some sense into him."

Rachel burst out laughing. "That's an interesting solution."

"I knew he didn't mean it. He was just panicking. The same way he panicked before taking Tina Beuller to the prom…the same way he panicked before going to Yale. He's that kind of guy."

"So obviously you talked him back into the wedding," she said, her attention moving back to the picture.

"Yeah. It didn't take more than about ten minutes. I got him to the church on time. Never did get all the tape off his tux, though."

"Sounds like you've got an interesting relationship," she commented.

"You could say that."

He and Craig had been rivals for most of their lives. From high school grades to girls they dated, the brothers had been neck and neck. And then they'd gone their separate ways. Matt started his firefighter training and Craig headed off to Yale Law School. Their rivalry got complicated then.

"But you're close?" Rachel asked, pulling him back to the present.

"Yeah, we have each other's backs." He shrugged. "He's blessed. He's got a good woman there."

"She's pretty."

"Yeah, but it's more than that. She understands him, and after totally figuring him out, she still wanted to marry him."

Rachel smiled. "Sounds like he had you working for that marriage, too."

"Gloria is intent on returning the favor and finding me a wife. She's the matchmaking type."

The coffee stopped sputtering and Matt turned back to the counter to pour coffee. He grabbed two mugs, both with fire-station logos across the side. He glanced back to find her still entranced by the information on his fridge. He shook his head wryly. Most people preferred to admire his backyard or the kitchen renovations, but Rachel was different.

"Who's this?" she asked, pointing to another photo. "Your parents?"

"That's them. They're retired in Arizona now."

"They look nice…"

"What about your parents?" he asked.

"They both passed away," she replied. "My aunt is the closest family I've got."

"I'm sorry to hear that."

She didn't answer but slowly turned away from the refrigerator and accepted the hot mug of taupe coffee with a smile of thanks. She took a slow sip, her long lashes brushing her cheeks as she closed her eyes in a sigh of contentment.

"You never did put down your roots here in Haggerston, did you?" she asked, her eyes popping open.

Matt blinked in surprise at the question. "What do you mean?"

"Well, I mean your brother is here with his wife, and you grew up in Haggerston, right?"

"Yeah, I did."

"You even knew my grandmother." She cradled the mug between her palms. "But this place doesn't have a hold on you."

He shrugged. "Sometimes that hold can feel claustrophobic."

She nodded and buried her nose in the mug once more, averting her gaze as she took another sip of coffee.

"I don't mean—" He stopped, uncertain how to even explain himself. "I'm not saying that a home and a family don't appeal."

"No?"

"Thing is, I don't have a family of my own here in Haggerston. My brother does. My cousins do. When you're younger you feel connected to a place for the extended family there. I guess I got to the point where I realized without a wife and kids of my own, it didn't matter as much."

"Always the single guy at the family picnic?" she asked with a wry smile.

"Pretty much." He laughed softly, but his heart felt heavy. Maybe he wasn't even the marrying type. It wasn't logical, he knew, but he hadn't been able to deliver Natalie Martin to her parents in time, and that had changed something inside him. If the Martins had lost their daughter because he'd been too late, did he deserve kids of his own after that? Maybe he was better off being the single, reliable guy, protecting the community and doing penance for his inability to protect little Natalie.

Except he wasn't even doing penance, was he? He was trying to move on the only way he knew how— getting out of Dodge.

"So, how about you?" he asked with a slow smile. "You're just as single as I am."

"True. So I can commiserate with being the only single one at a family picnic. It's lonely."

"So, why haven't you moved on yet?"

She wasn't the kind of woman who would stay single long, unless she wanted it that way. She was pretty, confident, had a smile that sparkled through her eyes—even he was intrigued, and he was determined to leave town.

"Chris couldn't handle it. Not yet." She grew serious. "Things have been hard enough for him without his mother starting to date. What he needs right now is some stability, and I'm going to provide that."

"I get it." He nodded slowly.

She shot him a teasing grin. "And as you pointed out so gently before, what I need right now are friends."

Maybe it was the testosterone pumping through his system, but that sounded like a veiled request for help, and for once, that was something he knew how to fix.

"I could help you out with that," he offered.

"You want to introduce me to some people?" she asked.

"I want to take you to my brother's barbecue tomorrow night." He glanced out the window at the rain. "Weather permitting, of course."

"Really? I don't want to put you out." She shook her head. "No, it's too much, Matt. We aren't your problem."

"You're wearing my clothes at the moment," he said

with a roguish grin. "That makes you at least partially my problem."

"But your brother might not like having a complete stranger crash his party."

"Are you kidding? They'll be thrilled to see me with a woman. In fact, if you do me a favor and don't tell Gloria that you've figured out what a lout I am, I could weasel out of her setups for a month at least. Besides, there will be a lot people there you'll want to meet."

Rachel laughed and shook her head. "My clothes should be dry—" She turned toward the laundry room, where the dryer rumbled softly.

"I'm serious. It's not a family affair. My brother is having some friends over. I know everyone. They're very nice and they'll all love you. Chris can play with the other kids. Maybe some of them will go to his school in the fall."

She turned back, her dark gaze resting on him thoughtfully as if she was internally debating. "Sure, that sounds really nice, Matt. Thank you."

"Not a problem. Are you hungry?"

"I've got to get back and pick up Chris from my aunt's place. I said I'd be back by now." She shook her head apologetically.

"Of course. Looks like the rain is letting up, too."

Outside the window, the rain had lightened to a drizzle and an errant ray of sunlight was already breaking through the cloud cover. The dryer buzzed and Rachel turned toward the doorway of the kitchen, her wet hair leaving damp patches on her shoulders. She disappeared into the laundry room and Matt turned back to the window.

He felt a surge of success that she'd accepted his invitation. It wasn't a date—they both knew that—but he still liked the idea of having her with him, somehow. Just as long as he didn't get attached.

That evening, Rachel sat on the porch next to Aunt Louise, a jug of iced tea between them. The shadows stretched long, and birds twittered their evening songs. Some kids still played in the street, although Christopher had been in bed for an hour already, and Rachel stretched her legs out and rested her head against the back of the Adirondack chair.

The day had taken its toll on her, and Rachel closed her heavy eyelids, breathing in the honeyed scent of rain-drenched lilacs. It was the same scent from the thunderstorm, and it brought back thoughts of Matt Bailey—his blue eyes clouded by complicated emotions and tension along his jawline, accentuating his rugged good looks.

"How is Chris doing…with the move and all?" Louise asked, taking a slow sip of the sweet brew.

Rachel's eyes fluttered open and she glanced toward her aunt. "I honestly don't know."

"He seems happy." Louise whisked a fly away from her glass.

"He always seemed happy enough." She deposited her glass on the table between them. "He'd laugh and play, and then I'd get a call from the school—"

Rachel's mind went back to the uncomfortable meetings with the principal and the school counselor. Chris was getting into fights, had learned some choice words that he spelled wrong but still insisted on writing all over his desk, and showed all the signs of a child in distress. She couldn't help feeling responsible, having just explained to him about his adoption. It was her fault, and she knew it. She'd explained everything too late.

"He isn't a bad kid," Louise said. "He's got a good heart, that boy."

"I think so, too." Rachel shot her aunt a smile.

"Isn't his birthday this month? We should do something fun."

"It was last month. We celebrated before we came."

"Did you have a proper party?" Louise pressed.

"We were moving," she said softly. "So, no. Not a proper one."

"We should have a birthday party for him here," Louise suggested. "A big family shindig. It might help him to feel more at home with us."

Rachel paused, mulling the idea over in her mind, and then she nodded. "That's actually a good idea."

"I'm full of them," Louise said with a grin. "And speaking of good ideas, what about our deputy fire chief?"

"What about him?" Rachel asked.

"You were at the fire station with him today…" Louise's eyes sparkled. "What do you think of him?"

She looked away, not wanting to share the details of their walk. Her aunt already knew too much, and for some reason, Rachel wanted to keep that sweet walk in the rain as a personal memory.

"He seems like a decent man," she said.

"And goodness knows a decent man is rare enough," Louise said with a pragmatic nod. She sipped her iced tea, flicking a pointed look over the top of her glass in Rachel's direction.

Rachel laughed. "I'm not looking for a boyfriend, Auntie."

"Who said anything about looking?" Louise shrugged exaggeratedly. "But if one were to fall into your lap—"

"Auntie, stop." Rachel laughed. "I'm serious. Even if a fabulous man dropped into my lap, I'm in no position to start dating. You know that."

"Actually I didn't know that." Louise turned toward Rachel, eyebrows raised. "Ed has been gone for almost five years now. Why not meet someone new?"

"It's only a little over four years," she said, correcting her aunt. "And I can't just start up with someone. I don't think Chris could handle it right now."

"A father figure might be good for him."

"A father figure, perhaps, but not a stepfather. He has enough to adjust to right now, what with discovering he was adopted and now the move to Haggerston. I came here to try to help Chris, and I can't get distracted right now."

Louise nodded. "I do understand that. Chris comes first. You do what you have to do for your children. I wanted to go back to work when Nickie started school, but she hated school, and I didn't want to add to her stress by adding a babysitter into the mix. You do what you have to do."

"Exactly," Rachel said. "Besides, I couldn't be with a firefighter again."

"I thought you were happy with Ed."

"I was."

"It isn't his fault he died."

"I know that." She shot her aunt a wry smile. "I married Ed not knowing what it meant to be a firefighter's wife. Well, now I know."

Louise nodded slowly. "Ignorance is bliss, my dear."

"No more firefighters." Rachel lifted her glass in a toast. "I don't think my heart could take it."

A bumblebee droned lazily above the flowers lining the walk, and Rachel's mind wandered back to her girlhood summers spent in this very house. Quiet evenings like this one had been the norm, and she and her grandmother would sit and talk. Their favorite conversations were about Rachel's "grown-up life," when they would try to imagine the beautiful life she had ahead of her.

"You'll meet a wonderful man," her grandmother would say. "He'll get to know you the proper way, and he'll fall in love with you."

"Why will he fall in love with me?"

"Because of your kind heart, of course," her grandmother would reply with a throaty laugh. "He'll ask you out to dinner, and he'll behave like a perfect gentleman. And after you've gotten to know each other, he'll get down on one knee and ask you to marry him. Then you'll call me up and tell me that you're engaged, and we'll all start planning your beautiful wedding day."

Her grandmother had always made her life sound like a fairy tale, full of romance and old-fashioned gestures. As a grown woman, she could see what her grandmother had been doing. She'd been trying to show Rachel what was possible if she followed God's plan.

Ed had been a loving and attentive husband. He was four inches shorter than she was, stocky and balding, and he'd treated her like the most beautiful woman in the world. Tears misted her eyes at the sweet memories, but those days were gone now, and here she was back in the rambling old house.

She was no longer a girl, and she had a child of her own now, but sitting on this stoop reminded her of her grandmother's predictions for the future, and despite her complicated situation, she couldn't help the hope that rose inside her.

Were her grandmother's predictions possible the second time around?

"I miss Grandma," Rachel said quietly.

"Me, too. She was the best mother-in-law a woman could ask for." Aunt Louise put her glass down on the table between them. "Have you been to her grave since you've been back?"

Rachel shook her head. "I've been so busy. I used to love reading all the inscriptions on the stones when I was young."

"I remember that." Aunt Louise smiled. "I'm going to help set up for a wedding shower on Wednesday at the church. Why don't you come along? You could show Chris the Emmett plots while I'm busy inside."

"Sure."

It might be good for Chris, too, Rachel thought. A birthday party could introduce him to his family here in town, and a little family-history lesson could introduce him to the family who had already passed away. Christopher belonged to more than just her. He had a whole family in Haggerston, and he belonged with the Emmetts, too. If only she could help him to see that.

Chapter Four

Craig and Gloria Bailey lived in an ordinary subdivision on the east side of Haggerston. It felt strange to walk through a stranger's home without being let in, but Matt sauntered ahead of her confidently enough. The pictures on their walls were from their wedding—loving looks, poses with the wedding party—and obviously some of Craig's bachelor decor hadn't been negotiated out of the house yet, as was evident by a mounted deer head leaning up against one living room wall and a yield sign beside it.

"I can tell that they're newlyweds," Rachel said, keeping her voice low. She glanced back to see that Chris was following close behind.

"Is it all the small appliances on the counter?" Matt asked as they entered the kitchen. Rachel had to admit that two toasters, a panini press and the three different sizes of blenders were probably a bit much, but all were likely wedding gifts.

"That, too," she admitted.

A half-open patio door separated them from the gathering outside. The din of voices and laughter flowed into the house with the warm summer breeze. As they stepped outside, a man waved from his position by the barbecue, and she recognized him from the wedding photo. The redheaded wife stood a few feet away, chatting with an older lady, and when she looked up and saw Matt standing next to Rachel, the woman's gaze flickered between them, and a smile spread over her face. She excused herself and headed in their direction.

"This is Gloria," Matt said before she got close enough to overhear. "You'll like her."

"Hello, hello!" Gloria gushed, hurrying up. "I'm glad you could make it. Craig did mention you were bringing a date—"

"No, not a date," Matt corrected with a chuckle. "This is Rachel Carter and her son, Christopher. They're new to Haggerston. They arrived, what—" He looked toward Rachel. "A couple of weeks ago."

"Well, welcome to town," Gloria said, beaming. She bent down and shook Christopher's hand. "We've got some Popsicles over there." She pointed to a little group of children on the far side of the yard. "Would you like me to introduce you to the other kids and find you a treat?"

Chris looked askance at Rachel and she nodded her permission. Gloria swept off with Chris in tow, and she cast a knowing smile over her shoulder in Matt's direction. He laughed softly.

"Sorry about that. She thinks she's giving us some time alone."

"Yeah, I got that." She grinned. "Can't fault her for trying."

"Hungry?" he asked.

"I am, actually."

They ambled toward the table laden with chips, salads and burger fixings. Rachel took a paper plate and dropped some potato chips, veggies and dip onto it. Her stomach rumbled.

"Hi, bro."

She glanced up to see Matt's brother heading in their direction. He wore a pair of khaki shorts and a pink polo shirt, a spatula in hand. Matt was taller, and his orange polo shirt strained slightly around his muscular arms, but the brothers seemed to have a lot in common, their fashion sense included. Craig nodded to Matt, then turned to Rachel.

"Hey, nice to have you here. I'm Craig, Matt's brother."

"Nice to meet you." She shook his hand. "I'm Rachel. I'll be teaching at Broxton Park Elementary this September."

"Yeah, Matt mentioned. There are a few teachers here today, and I'm sure Matt can make some introductions. Can I get you two a burger?"

"That would be great, thanks," Matt replied, and Rachel nodded her assent.

"You want your burger well-done, right?" Craig called over his shoulder as he headed back toward the barbecue, but he didn't stop for the answer.

"The teachers he mentioned are just over there." Matt pointed across the grass to a group of chatting people, plates in hand. "Actually all four of them. The man over there in the yellow T-shirt is a pediatrician. He's a good guy to know. The woman he's talking to is an orthodontist here in town. Oh, and that short woman with the baby is one of the librarians..."

Rachel felt her earlier perkiness waning. She was here to meet other people, and he was here to make that happen. She pushed away her unwarranted disappointment and forced a smile to her lips.

Welcome back to reality, she thought wryly.

"I'll go over and introduce myself," she said.

"Do you want me to come with you?" he asked.

"Oh, why start the tongues wagging? I'll be fine."

He nodded, and she thought she detected some disappointment in his eyes, too. "Great. Have a good time."

Of course, she knew that nothing could happen between herself and Matt, but she couldn't deny the spark between them—a spark that it might be smarter to stamp out before either of them got hurt.

Chris stood next to another boy about the same size, both with a frosty Popsicle in hand. They looked amiable enough, and she let her gaze linger on her son. He stood there with that stance of vulnerable bravery that children had when they felt uncertain about themselves, and she sighed softly.

Lord, she prayed for the thousandth time, *show me what he needs.*

Before Chris could catch her watching him, which he seemed to hate lately, Rachel angled her steps toward the group of chatting teachers. When she stopped next to them, they continued talking, taking no notice of her. Her own latent insecurity roused itself, and she pushed it back down.

"Hi," she said cheerfully. "I've been told you're all teachers."

The conversation stopped abruptly, and they all turned to look at her in mild surprise.

"Yes, we are," one woman said with a smile. She was plump and blonde with kind eyes. She wore a floral-patterned sundress. "Are you a parent?"

"I am. My son is going to be in the second grade this September," Rachel replied. "I'm also teaching fourth grade at Broxton Park."

"Are you really?" She beamed. "I'm teaching second grade at Broxton Park."

Rachel's heart soared momentarily with relief. This woman looked kind, understanding—the kind of teacher she'd prayed for, both for her son and as a colleague. "Oh, that's fantastic. He's just over there…" She pointed out Chris, who was now tucking in to a bowlful of potato chips, the Popsicle just starting to drip from the other hand. "This is a big transition for him."

"It would be. I'm Glenda, by the way." She shot out a hand and Rachel shook it heartily. The others smiled and shook her hand, introducing themselves.

So this will be home, she thought to herself as she listened to the teachers chat and laugh. It felt good. It felt right.

She glanced back in Matt's direction and found his eyes locked on her. She met his gaze in mild surprise. A smile twitched at one side of his lips, and he gave her a bashful smile, then turned away.

If she weren't mistaken, Matt was interested in her.

He's leaving, she reminded herself. *Don't let this get complicated.*

Matt held out his plate while his brother put a hamburger patty on top of his open bun. It was a good turnout for Craig's annual barbecue, and he had to admit that his brother knew how to entertain. Haggerston was a barbecue and cider kind of town.

"So you're serious?" Craig asked. "You have no intention of dating her?"

"Sorry. If all goes according to plan, I'm moving to South Maitland in a few months," he replied.

"She'd be worth sticking around for."

Matt glanced back in Rachel's direction at the same time that she swung her gaze toward him. Her hair, now smoothed back to the big, glossy waves she normally wore, swung down in front of one eye, and she pushed it back, at the same time shielding her eyes from the sun. The first image to pop into his mind was his memory of her standing in his foyer, dripping with rain, her hair springing up into her natural curl. Their eyes locked for a moment, and he pushed down the unbidden memory. He smiled uncomfortably and turned back to his brother.

"She's not interested."

"Oh, well, in that case." Craig shot him a teasing grin.

"I thought you were the one telling me not to get any hopes up," Matt retorted.

"Yeah, well…"

"It's not a good idea—you know that," he said.

"And if you don't get this job?" Craig prodded.

"She's still not interested." Matt shot his brother a victorious grin, as if having a cute brunette completely uninterested in what he had to offer were a good thing.

Craig craned his neck around to look in Rachel's direction again, and Matt refused to follow suit. Instead he grabbed some ketchup and started a slow coil on top of his burger.

"Looks like Allan just introduced himself," Craig said.

Matt grimaced. Allan Hennick, a real-estate agent, had gone to high school with Matt and Craig. He was successful, lived on a large acreage outside town and was known for his smooth ways around women. Matt couldn't stand him.

"Doesn't he have a woman in his life yet?" Matt muttered.

"Seems to me, he's working on it." Craig retorted.

Matt glanced back. Allan stood close to Rachel—close enough that she had to tip her head back to look him in the face. Allan said something and Rachel's laugh floated up over the conversation. Matt groaned inwardly.

Allan was known for sleeping around and moving on to the next conquest in record time—most of which happened during his marriage, resulting in a rather messy divorce.

"She's a grown woman," Matt said tersely.

"A grown woman who doesn't know that Allan's stint in the military lasted all of three weeks before he flunked out of boot camp," his brother said.

Craig turned to serve more burger patties to some guests, and Matt looked back in Rachel's direction. Allan plucked something—probably an imaginary something—out of Rachel's hair and she stepped back. Allan closed the distance again without missing a beat.

Anger bubbled up inside Matt's chest. Rachel was different—she was vulnerable, sweet and definitely too good to be toyed around with by the likes of Allan Hennick. He put down his plate, and before he'd even formulated a proper plan of action, he sauntered over in their direction, murmuring his excuses to the people he passed.

Allan was midstory when Matt arrived; the smaller man's gaze flickered momentarily in his direction.

"So, long story short," Allan was saying, "that's how I got this scar."

"Which scar is that, Allan?" Matt asked with a pointed smile.

"Don't worry about it," Allan replied smoothly. "The story's already over."

"That's amazing, Allan," Rachel said with a shake of her head. "I had no idea that snakes could do that."

"Snakes?" Matt raised an eyebrow. "We don't have too many around here."

Allan met Matt's gaze, and he shot him an irritated look. "Rachel and I were just talking..." Allan let the words hang in the air, the implication clear.

Matt nodded sagely, ignoring the rebuff. "You'll have to tell me that story one of these days. It's good to see you, Allan. How is your mother?"

"Fine. How is yours?"

"Oh, she's great. I heard that your mom wasn't doing so well lately and that she was going to move in with you."

It was a valid rumor that had spread all over town in the past week. Allan's mother had been angling to move in with her only son for years, and when she broke her ankle, it looked as though she might get her wish—for a few weeks, at least.

Allan smiled tightly at Matt. "She's doing just fine." He turned his attention toward Rachel, his smile softening. "I have to say, my large home on seven acres of land does get rather lonely on my own, though."

Matt curbed the urge to roll his eyes and crossed his arms over his broad chest. He was a good six inches taller than Allan, and he kept his gaze trained on the smaller man, who eyed him in annoyance.

"So, what do you do for a living, Rachel?" Allan asked, refocusing his attention on Rachel.

"I'll be teaching fourth grade at Broxton Park," she replied.

"Broxton Park?" Allan arched an eyebrow in Matt's direction. "Tragic fire there."

Matt's expression froze. That crossed a line.

"Yes." Rachel's sweet smile slipped and she eyed Allan with momentary distaste. "But that was in the past, and this is now. I'm sure everything is safe and up to code."

Allan cleared his throat. "I didn't mean to imply—" He shrugged apologetically. "You'll be very safe, I'm sure. In fact, if you wanted someone to show you around, as a real-estate agent—"

"Are you looking to buy right now?" Matt interrupted, looking toward Rachel with exaggerated innocence.

"No," she replied with a shake of her head, amusement flickering in her dark eyes. "I'm happy with where we are at the moment."

"Even if you aren't looking to buy—" Allan began.

"Isn't that your ex-wife?" Matt looked toward the house, where a woman was coming out onto the deck. She was heavily pregnant and had a two-year-old in tow. She was remarried already, and the expected baby belonged to her new husband. Matt felt slightly bad for pulling such a cheap shot, and Allan glared at Matt balefully.

"Hey, it's really good to see you, Allan," Matt said with a smile. "Rachel, I wanted to introduce you to someone."

Matt put a hand on her elbow and steered her away from the fuming Allan. Allan stomped off in the opposite direction, staying well clear of his ex-wife. Matt stifled the laugh that rose up inside him and angled her back toward the table of food.

"Who did you want to introduce me to?" Rachel asked, and Matt looked down at her in surprise.

"Anyone, really," he admitted ruefully. "But first, I thought you could probably use something to eat."

"I'll forgive you because you've brought me to the dessert table," she conceded, "but I have the distinct impression that you and Allan aren't friends."

"He's a toad," Matt said. "And he's got a bit of a reputation."

"For being a flirt and a womanizer?" Rachel asked, plucking a cupcake out of an arrangement and depositing it on her plate.

"Exactly. How did you know?"

"I'm not a naive girl," she replied with a low laugh. "I'm a grown woman. I've been married. I've met his type before, you know."

Of course, she was completely capable of taking care of herself. She'd already been married, and she probably knew more about relationships than he did. Heat rose in his neck and he shrugged apologetically.

"Sorry. I got a bit protective there. So, should I make good on my offer and introduce you to some people with decent reputations?"

She shook her head. "No, but you can pass me one of those brownies."

She pointed to a plate of thick, dark squares, and he took a napkin and nabbed the biggest brownie on top of the pile, placing it on her plate.

"Hungry?" he asked with a smile.

She shook her head. "Chris's favorite."

And with those words, the moment sagged. Of course,

none of this changed the reality of the situation, and they both knew it. He looked in the direction of the kids, and he noticed the boy standing off by himself, his eyes sad and dull. Chris's blond hair ruffled in the warm breeze, and he looked idly over the fence into the neighbor's yard, ignoring the other children who were playing in a flower bed.

Rachel flashed him a quick smile and angled in her son's direction. Matt stood back and watched as she bent down and revealed the treat on her paper plate. Chris perked up a little at the sight of the brownie, but even with his mother at his side, he looked alone.

Poor kid, Matt thought. *He's been through a lot.*

The one thing Matt was certain of was that if you wanted to protect a child, you had to protect the mother. And even though Rachel didn't seem inclined toward being protected, Matt wasn't going to let anyone take advantage of her on his watch.

"Looks like you lost out, too."

Matt looked over in surprise to find Allan at his elbow. Allan crossed his arms over his chest, standing a few inches into Matt's personal space—an obvious challenge. The smaller man's eyes were trained on Rachel, too, irritation still etched over his features.

"Yeah," Matt admitted with a wry grin, nodding toward the boy. "But this time it was to the better man."

Allan narrowed his eyes, then shook his head. "All right. I'll give you that. He looks like a cute kid. I could get used to him."

"Leave her alone." Matt dropped the smile, his tone low and steely.

Allan shot him an incredulous look. "Why? You have no claim on her."

"Because I care." Matt eyed him grimly. "I care about her and I care about that little boy. If I hear that you've messed with her the way you've done other women in this town, you'll have me to deal with. Personally."

Allan swallowed and took a step back. "Are you threatening me?"

"Hardly. Just telling it like it is. Leave her alone."

"Fine." Allan muttered something under his breath and walked away in the opposite direction. Matt watched him go. He had a feeling Rachel wouldn't approve of his Neanderthal methods, but he thought he could live with that. He might not be able to do much more for her, but he could keep one creep away from her, and that was something.

The next day, Matt flicked off the Saturday morning news and sauntered into his kitchen. He stared into the fridge for a minute, then shut it without taking anything out. He normally relished a quiet day to himself since they were so few and far between, but today his mind kept wandering back to Rachel. He felt mildly foolish for getting protective of her the day before. She was obviously capable of taking care of herself, but that hadn't completely quelled his urge to put Allan in his place.

Matt leaned against the counter and picked up a cup of warm coffee. He downed it in two gulps.

One question nagged at him: If it had been some other guy chatting up Rachel, would it have made a difference? He liked to think it might have, but if he had to be completely honest with himself, it wouldn't. Not really. What he'd felt was a protective instinct watered down with a big dose of jealousy.

He'd been planning on calling her this morning, but

he hadn't quite built up his courage yet. He was going to do a community fire-safety presentation at a church in a few days. He'd been told that it was being put on by the youth group, so that meant that the majority of the audience would be young, and he figured it would be a good opportunity for him to put some of Rachel's tips into action—and for her to coach him, if she was willing. Except he was slightly embarrassed now that he'd gotten all protective of her, and he was afraid she'd think he was asking for something more.

His phone rang and Matt pulled it out of his pocket, recognizing Rachel's number. He breathed a sigh of relief that she'd called first, and he picked up.

"Hi there," he said, a smile warm in his voice.

"Hi, Matt." Something clattered in the background, and Rachel's voice became muffled for a moment, and then she came back. "I'm sorry. What a morning over here! I was just calling to see if you know of a good plumber."

"That's not a good sign."

"No, not really," she agreed. "The only bathtub in the house is plugged right up, and I need to get someone in here to fix it."

"Just a plugged drain?" Matt asked. "Nothing more complicated than that?"

"You wouldn't say 'just a plugged drain' if you saw it," she retorted. "It's a mess!"

"I can fix that for you this morning."

"Do you moonlight as a plumber?"

"No, but I've fixed it in my own home enough times. It's not that complicated. Just takes a few tools. But if you don't trust me, I'll give you my uncle Sid's number."

Rachel laughed. "To vouch for you?"

"No, he's the best plumber in Haggerston, but I've got an advantage over him."

"Which is?"

"I'm free."

"You make a compelling case. You said you can come today?"

"For sure. Today is my day off, so I can be there in about an hour, if that works."

"Thank you, Matt." Something clattered in the background again. "You're a lifesaver. I'll see you soon."

Three-quarters of an hour later, Matt pulled up in front of Rachel's house. A curtain fluttered out an open window on the upper level, and from deep inside the house, the tinny jangle of a radio sang out a country tune. Chris sat alone on the front steps, a cracked, empty flowerpot in front of him and a stick in one hand. He glanced up as Matt parked the truck, and dropped his gaze again.

Matt hopped out of the truck, slamming the door with a bang. He'd brought some of the notes Rachel had given him about presentations along with him, just in case, and he folded the page lengthwise and shoved it into his back pocket.

"Hi, buddy," Matt said as he ambled up the path.

Chris didn't answer. Matt stood next to him for a long moment, undecided, then dropped his tool belt onto the wooden steps with a clunk and sank down next to him. The boy didn't want to talk, and Matt didn't feel the need to change that. Instead he picked up a pebble and tossed it toward the flowerpot. He missed.

Chris picked up another pebble and tossed it. It rattled into the ceramic pot, and Chris shot him a victorious grin.

"Nice shot," Matt muttered.

Matt tossed another pebble, this time landing it perfectly. He couldn't be beaten by a seven-year-old. His adult ego just couldn't take it.

Chris grabbed another little rock and the game was on. They tossed stones, each mentally keeping score, the only sounds that of the click of pebble hitting ceramic. Chris's small shoulders relaxed and the brooding look in his eyes slowly seeped away, leaving the determined glint of a boy who wanted to win. Sometimes a guy needed to compete in order to hammer out his conflicting feelings, and little boys were no different from their full-grown counterparts.

The day after the Broxton Park Elementary fire, Matt had played basketball with his brother, not stopping until they both were slick with sweat and breathing hard. He'd slammed basket after basket, ramming his own pain and frustration through the hoop with the ball. He'd beaten out his grief with his shoes against pavement until he had no more strength to give.

The fix wasn't permanent, but it was therapeutic.

Craig was the kind of brother who could play basketball with you and never say a word about the elephant in the room. Sometimes a man just needed to stare down his elephant alone. It looked as though a kid needed that luxury, too. At least today.

Chris threw another pebble and landed it perfectly.

"Nice," Matt said and stuck out a foot, pushing the pot farther back. "Let's try that."

Chris shot Matt a grin. The challenge was accepted.

Chapter Five

Rachel stood in the open doorway, her hand on the screen door. Matt sat on the steps with Chris, their backs to her. Matt's strong, muscular back made Chris's slender form seem all the smaller in comparison, yet they both sat in a similar stance, hunched over in concentration as they tossed pebbles at a cracked flowerpot. In a wash of summer sunlight, sitting on the sagging front steps, they were just two guys throwing rocks. She was about to push the door open but didn't have the heart to interrupt them.

She'd spent the morning planning Chris's birthday party for the next week. When she'd told Chris about Aunt Louise's idea, he'd been initially excited and then uncertain.

"But who will come?" he'd asked.

"Everyone. Aunt Louise, Uncle Herb, Uncle Chet, Aunt Joanne—"

"I don't know Uncle Chet."

"Yes, you do. You met him at Aunt Louise's house. He's the one with the motorcycle."

"Oh, yeah." He'd brightened at the mention of the motorcycle.

"Everyone wants to get to know us better," she'd explained. "And a kid only turns seven once."

She felt desperately hopeful about this party. A day of balloons and cake couldn't fix everything, but she hoped that it would be the start of a few roots in his young life—a memory he could look back on when he was grown and could say *Remember that party we had in Grandma Rose's old house?*

On the front step, Chris's pebble dropped into the center of the pot, and Rachel found herself beaming in spite of herself. It was a good shot. Matt glanced over at Chris and gave him a nod of respect.

The floor squeaked as Rachel shifted her weight, and Matt turned, his blue eyes meeting hers with a smile.

"You're here," she said.

"Sorry, I got caught up in a very serious competition here."

"I noticed." She chuckled.

"I lost," he admitted ruefully.

"By three," Chris added helpfully, and Rachel smothered a laugh.

"Actually by four, I think," Matt said. "Good game, Chris."

Matt lifted a tool belt from the step beside him and rose to his feet. Chris bounced up next to him, and Rachel felt a wave of relief at her son's enthusiasm. Lately, anything that made him happy made her hope that they were turning a corner.

"Upstairs?" Matt paused and looked down into her face. His clear eyes held her gaze for a beat longer than necessary before she answered.

"Yes, upstairs, first door on the left."

A smile flickered at the corners of his lips. "Let's see if I can fix this."

Rachel dropped her gaze and jogged up the stairs in front of him, leading the way to the malfunctioning tub.

The bathroom was nothing extraordinary—a sink, a beveled mirror and a tub. Rachel remembered rinsing mud from her face and hair in this very bathroom after a mud fight with a cousin twenty years earlier. She'd had a good cry in that bathroom when she felt homesick for her parents but didn't want Grandma to know about it. She'd lounged in that tub as a girl, wondering what it would be like to be a "grown-up lady." That bathroom hadn't changed—not even the cracked tile beside the tub.

"It drains very, very slowly," she explained. "I've tried those liquid drain cleaners, and nothing seems to work."

Matt dropped his tools onto the floor and squatted next to the tub. He grabbed a wrench and set to work dismantling the drain. As his hands moved, his muscles flexing as he strained against the stubborn plumbing, he shot her a boyish grin. "I'm sorry about yesterday. I shouldn't have gotten all Neanderthal on you."

"Oh, that's no problem," she assured him. "I actually got a call from Allan this morning."

She hadn't been entirely thrilled to hear from him, especially since she wasn't sure how he'd gotten her number. When she'd asked him about it, he'd said that he'd overheard her give her number to one of the teachers, something she hadn't liked. It seemed creepy.

"Oh?" Matt's gaze flickered up toward her, then back down to his work.

"He asked me out to dinner," she admitted.

Matt pulled up the inside of the drain, the whole

piece, including the dripping clog, coming up together in a greasy, slimy mess.

"Ew." Rachel peered over his shoulder, wincing in embarrassment. "I'm sorry. I feel like I should be politely hiding that from you. That's nasty."

"It was formed well before you arrived," Matt said. "Got a garbage?" Matt shook the clog into the garbage and glanced up at Rachel speculatively. "And?"

"And what?" she asked.

"Are you going out with him?"

Rachel felt the smile tickle at her lips. "No."

Matt nodded, and some of the tension eased out of his shoulders. He cared—that much was clear. He didn't want her to go out with Allan, and while she could see that Allan was most definitely a cad, she found Matt's protectiveness endearing.

"See?" Matt said. "Clog fixed. Easy peasy."

"You are pretty handy after all," she said.

"You sound surprised." He shot her a grin.

"Well, a girl can never be too sure. To listen to Allan, he's a war hero and a business genius. Sometimes guys exaggerate their abilities," she teased.

"Do they, now?" Matt began reassembling the drain, fitting the pieces back together. "Not me. If I say I can do it, I can." He arched an eyebrow at her teasingly. "And if I say I'm terrible at something, you can trust that, too."

"And what are you terrible at?" she asked.

He thought for a moment as he tightened the last part, then rinsed off his hands. "I'm a terrible singer."

"Oh, you can't be that bad." She grinned.

"Sure can." He laughed. "And apparently I'm not good at warning women away from Allan with any measure of grace or dignity."

Rachel rewarded him with a spontaneous laugh. "I actually appreciate it. I'm used to taking care of everyone else. It's nice to have someone looking out for me for a change."

Matt stood up and dropped his tools back into the belt. "Done."

"Thank you, Matt. I really appreciate this. Can I get you some lemonade or something?"

"Sure, that would be great."

"Do you want some lemonade, too, Chris?" Rachel called into the hallway.

From a bedroom, Chris called back, "No, I'm playing now."

Rachel led the way downstairs and into the kitchen. She gestured toward the old kitchen table and Matt sank into a chair while she grabbed two tall glasses and a pitcher of pink lemonade from the fridge.

"I was going to mention it earlier," Matt said as he took a seat. He pulled some folded sheets of paper from his back pocket. "I'm doing a fire-safety presentation for a local church. Would you be free to critique me?"

She nodded. "Which evening?"

"Friday."

That was still several days away, and Rachel did a quick mental tally. She and Aunt Louise had plans to swing by Peace Hills Christian Church on Wednesday. Friday, however, would be free.

"I could arrange for Chris to be with my aunt Friday evening. I don't see a problem."

"Thanks." He shot her a smile. "Do you want a ride?"

"Sure." She smiled back. "What time should I expect you?"

"Well, the presentation starts at seven, so I'd say about six-thirty."

Overhead, Chris thumped as he played a game upstairs, and a mild summer breeze wafted through an open window carrying the scent of lilacs. The kitchen tap drip-drip-dripped in a lazy staccato. Even the clock above the kitchen entryway seemed to slow down the seconds in that hazy summer day, slowing down her inner rhythms. Rachel leaned silently forward, refilling his glass with ice-cold lemonade, and she caught his eye with a friendly smile.

"I only have one concern," Rachel said quietly.

"What's that?"

"Well, you and I both know that you aren't planning on being around here too much longer. I haven't told Chris that because seven-year-olds aren't very discreet, if you know what I mean."

"I have an idea."

"I know I wanted you and Chris to get to know each other, but I don't want Chris to get hurt."

"When—if—I leave."

She nodded. "He's been through so much lately, and I want him to settle in here. I just don't want him to get too attached to you and then have him be heartbroken when you move away."

He nodded. "I get it. So I should keep my distance a bit."

"Yes and no." She searched his face, hoping that he understood. "I think his relationship with you is really important. Just be careful. He's a sensitive boy."

She didn't want to offend him, but she knew that if she didn't protect her son's little heart, no one else in the world would. He had that combination of strength and fragility that all children had, but right now he was a little more fragile than most.

"Okay," Matt said with a curt nod. "I'll do my best."

"Thank you."

Rachel had just complicated things further, and she knew it, but a mother's job was a pricklier experience than she'd ever appreciated before. His birthday party was coming up, and it was a good opportunity for Chris to start building some bonds with the people who would be staying in his life. Besides, Rachel found herself getting closer and closer to this firefighter, and it would be better for everyone if they could just keep this professional. When Matt eventually left, it would be hard for Chris, and if she could make that goodbye easier, she would. It would probably be better if Matt weren't invited to this party.

"I thought of another technique you might find helpful," she suggested, changing the subject. "Since you're here."

"Thanks. I appreciate it." He pulled his page of notes closer. "And, Rachel, I really will be careful with Chris. I don't want to hurt him, either."

She smiled her thanks. He understood, and that would make things easier.

Wednesday arrived, and Rachel and Aunt Louise loaded Chris into the car and headed out to the church. Peace Hills Cemetery had no hills. It was nestled behind the Peace Hills Christian Church just outside town, a steepled church in the middle of a verdant field. All around, the land rolled out flat and empty, except for the distant farms and the slow, passive cows that chewed their cud just past the barbed-wire fence that separated church property from farmland. The old-fashioned church stood along a solitary stretch of highway, a single-story building, the white siding blasted by the weather down to gray boards. Every few years, during the hot summer months, the members would donate time and resources to bring the faded old building back to a gleaming white. During her summer visits to Haggerston in her youth, Rachel and her grandmother had helped in painting the church twice that Rachel could remember.

It seemed right that Grandma Rose rested here in the cemetery behind the church that had been the center of her life.

"Do you remember Grandma Rose?" Rachel asked her son.

Chris surveyed the graveyard and shook his head. "No."

"Well, you were pretty little when you last saw her. You were about three and a half, I think."

"And this is hers?" He squatted next to the marble gravestone, engraved with Rose Emmett's birth and death, followed by a Bible verse.

"This is hers." Rachel looked down at the grave sadly. "I miss her a lot. She was a great lady. She thought you were a pretty special kid, too, you know."

Christopher looked to the grave next to hers. "And that's Grandpa's?"

"Yes, that's Grandpa. Well, my grandfather, and your great-grandfather. He died about twenty years ago. And over here…" Rachel led the way through the gravestones to an old, chipped stone. "This is your great-great-grandfather's gravestone. And next to his is his first wife, Lily. His second wife was buried in a different graveyard with her family."

"So this is our family?"

"This is a lot of them," Rachel replied.

"What about Dad?"

"He's buried in Billings."

"Shouldn't he be here, too?"

Rachel sighed. "We buried him where we lived. We did the best we could."

"They're not really my family, though," Chris said. "Not really, right?"

"Of course they're your family." Rachel squatted down next to her son. "Why would you say that?"

"Jeremy at school said that my real family didn't want me. That's what being adopted means."

"No, being adopted means that your biological mom gave you to us, to be our son. You're Christopher Carter, and this *is* your family. We want you very much." Her voice quivered, and she looked earnestly into his blue eyes.

"Yeah." He lacked enthusiasm.

"Sometimes other kids will say things that are pretty dumb," she said. "They don't know what they're talking about."

"Okay."

This was an old conversation. They'd had it several times already, and she'd hoped that by bringing him to this graveyard, showing him the generations of Emmetts, he might feel more of a connection to the family line.

"Look." She brushed her hand over the top of a gravestone. "This is your great-great-grandfather's grave. He was an army pilot. He flew planes."

The graveyard circled around the side of the building, and Rachel angled her steps in that direction, her son walking along behind her. The high-noon sunlight beat down on their heads and Rachel headed closer to the church for the slim line of shade next to the building.

"What's over here?" Christopher asked.

"Run ahead and see," she replied.

Chris picked up his pace and jogged around the corner. As she walked on, her heart sank heavily. She kept bringing him to places that held her childhood memories, hoping to somehow share the strength that she had found here, only to fall short every time. This church loomed tall and cheerful in her mind, yet for Chris, it seemed to be nothing more than an aged building. The gravestones that had sparked her imagination when she was a girl seemed to remind her own son that he wasn't biologically linked to the family that rested beneath them.

Lord, he's my child, but other people keep telling him otherwise. How do I fix this?

As she rounded the corner, she stopped short. Chris stood next to an angel statue, his hand resting on one outstretched wing. Beyond him, Matt Bailey crouched next to a small headstone at the other side of the graveyard. It was situated by the corner of the graveyard fence, a line of lilac bushes sheltering it from the prairie wind. He sat motionless on the balls of his feet, shoulders slumped. He was a big man—well built and solid.

"Who's that?" Chris whispered.

"Someone who's come to visit a grave," she replied softly, not wanting to interrupt Matt's quiet moment.

Chris was accustomed to graveyard visits. She used to take him quite often to her late husband's resting place, but he seemed entranced by this figure of solitary grief.

Chris moved in Matt's direction and Rachel made a swipe for his shoulder to redirect him, but missed. She jogged after the boy and caught his shoulder a few feet behind Matt's crouched form, tugging Chris back.

"No, Chris," she whispered. "People need privacy."

Matt glanced back, mildly surprised to see them.

"Hey, it's Mr. Bailey!" Chris announced with a grin.

"I'm sorry to intrude," she said with an apologetic smile.

"It's okay." Matt cleared his throat and rose to his feet. "How are you doing?"

"Not too badly." A breeze lifted Rachel's hair and she brushed it away from her face with a bat of her hand. It felt strange to be standing here making conversation, pretending that they weren't standing in the middle of a graveyard. Graveyards were personal places where people sat with their grief, and no one knew that better than she. Discomfort warmed her cheeks. "I just brought Chris by for a little family history lesson."

"That sounds like a good idea," Matt said, his voice low.

Chris crouched down in the same spot Matt had occupied only moments ago and examined the small stone with solemn attention.

"Who's this?" Chris asked, reaching out to reverently touch the flat stone.

"That's a little girl who died a few years ago." Matt cleared his throat.

"Is she your little girl?" Chris asked, and Rachel found herself holding her breath, waiting for the reply.

"No. She was…" He scrubbed a hand through his hair. "She was a friend."

"Oh." Chris pointed across the graveyard. "Our family is just over there."

Rachel felt a swell of relief at her son's words *our family*. Matt's eyes followed Chris's pointing finger.

"The graves," Rachel explained, just in case Matt was expecting to see a group of living Emmetts, and Matt nodded again.

"Matt, I'm sorry to disturb you," she said quietly. "We'll give you some privacy."

"No, no." Matt shook his head. "I don't mean to be rude. This…" He looked toward the grave once more. "She died in the Broxton Park Elementary School fire."

"Oh…" The breath seeped out of her and Rachel looked from Matt to the tiny grave and back again. "You knew her?" she asked cautiously.

"No. Yes." He sighed. "I tried to save her."

"Oh, Matt…" Rachel put a hand on his well-muscled forearm. Chris headed back in the direction of his grandparents' graves, and Rachel dropped her hand. The big man seemed to be shouldering more weight than she could imagine, and his face, chiseled into a granite mask, didn't hide the pain in his eyes.

"I'd better go with Chris," she said quietly. "We'll give you privacy."

"I wouldn't mind the company, actually."

"Do you want to come check out a few generations of Emmetts?" she asked.

"Sure."

As they walked through the graveyard toward the other side of the church, some chickadees chattered in the bushes, and a hawk circled slowly overhead. A gentle breeze carried the scent of flowers over the sleepy graveyard, and Rachel paused to look up at the stained-glass windows. These were the windows at the back of the church that would appear over the choir stall for parishioners inside, and they depicted an image of the resurrection. The tomb gaped open with the stone rolled back, and a haloed angel stood next to it. Women with heads covered crouched to one side, hands raised in surprise or a symbolic gesture of piety, Rachel wasn't sure which.

Matt's gaze was directed away from the old church building, past the graveyard with the protective shrubbery surrounding it, to the expanse of pasture beyond where the grass rippled in the prairie breeze. She caught the restless sadness flickering in those dark eyes, and again, she felt as though the things that comforted her failed to comfort the people with her.

The side door to the church opened, and Aunt Louise poked her head out.

"I need a big strong boy to help me set up some chairs, Chris," she called cheerily. "And I have some fresh cupcakes for when we're done…"

Chris looked askance at his mother and she smilingly waved him inside.

Cupcakes could lift any mood for a small boy. She wished it were so easy once they grew up.

The side door of the church shut with a bang and Matt glanced toward the pretty brunette. The wind ruffled through her glossy hair and fluttered the pale pink blouse around her slim waist. She was looking at him, her dark eyes thoughtful. He'd said more than he'd planned to, and the knowledge left him uneasy.

"So, what about these Emmetts?" he asked in an attempt to change the subject.

"Aunt Louise is one of them." A smile toyed at her lips. "Forget the Emmetts. What about you?"

"My family?"

"No, you." She met his gaze easily. "I've lost a husband, so I know a thing or two about grieving. It helps to talk."

"I don't tend to talk about it."

"Why not?" She moved away from him, toward the crumbling graves at the rear, and he found himself following her before he even thought about it.

"Everyone in this town had to grieve the loss of that little girl," he said. "Some things are best left alone."

"Well, I'm a stranger—almost." She glanced up at him. "It won't hurt me to hear this like it might someone who knew her."

"You know what happened," he said gruffly, hoping she'd be put off by his tone, but her expression didn't change.

"Not really." She shrugged. "I know there was a fire—"

He sighed. She was determined—he'd give her that. "It was a big one. It spread faster than anyone anticipated."

"What caused it?"

"Arson."

They stopped at a stone bench beside a scraggly rosebush. A few blooms adorned the thorny branches, and the leaves wilted from lack of rainfall. Whoever set up this spot had probably envisioned a beautiful little corner where someone could sit in the aroma of roses like in some British fantasy, but the reality of the situation included Montana weather. A stunted rosebush and a bench were as good as this was going to get. He sat down, staring at his shoes for a long moment. Rachel's silky blouse brushed against his arm as she sank down next to him. The sun slipped behind a cloud, the warm day perceptibly cooling. He wasn't sure he even wanted to talk about this, but he found the words coming out of his mouth before he could stop them.

"I was in charge of fighting that fire."

"So you feel responsible."

"I *was* responsible. All the students had been evacuated from the school but one. No one could find her, and after the men came out exhausted, I suited up and went in." He shook his head slowly. "I can still remember the sound of her parents crying on the sidewalk."

"But you did find her."

"Yeah, I did. She was scared. A big fireman in uniform can be really terrifying for kids, and she was only five—one of the kindergartners. I almost missed her, but I saw her shoe sticking out from behind a garbage can, and I guess I came up too quickly. I was focused on getting her out of there—she'd already been in there so long—and she was trying to get away from me."

"Is that common?"

"It can be. That's why we go into every school in town and show the kids how our equipment works. We don't want them to be afraid of a firefighter. Anyway, she kept trying to run away, and the smoke was getting thicker. By the time I spotted her shoe behind that garbage can, she was barely conscious…" Matt stopped, swallowed hard. "I got her out, but by the time I got her outside…" He cleared his throat. "She'd been burned quite badly. She never did wake up."

Rachel stretched her legs out in front of her, and when he glanced over, he found her dark eyes locked on him. "Was this girl the first person to die in a fire here?" she asked softly.

"No."

"But she's the hardest?"

Matt didn't know how to put all this into words. He'd rescued an old woman several years earlier who had died of her burns in the hospital. He'd personally pulled a young man out of the wreckage of a car and performed CPR on him for five minutes before the ambulance arrived, only to discover he had died on impact. He'd seen horrible things and been there as the emergency response, but Natalie Martin was different.

"She was the first child," he said finally.

Rachel nodded. "Kids…" Her chin trembled. "It makes it different, doesn't it?"

"Yeah."

"Do you stay in touch with the family?"

Matt frowned down at the ground. "No. I don't need to keep reminding them about that day."

"I'm sure they remember anyway."

"Yeah, well…" He took a deep breath and met her gaze. "I wouldn't know what to say. And I doubt it would make any of us feel any better." He'd already said too much.

They were silent for a couple of minutes, the breeze shifting her hair ever so slightly. He liked the quiet—it didn't require anything of him, and he could just sit here with this beautiful woman at his side. She glanced up at him.

"I remember being so angry with Ed. He had a habit of turning his phone off and completely forgetting to turn it back on. It drove me crazy, and that night, I'd been trying to reach him for hours, and Christopher was already in bed asleep. I was furious with him. Then the police knocked at my door with the news that he was dead."

Matt winced. "Do you feel guilty for being mad at him?"

"No, not anymore." She shook her head. "Sometimes I'm still mad at him for dying, though."

"Inconsiderate." He shot her a sad smile.

"Completely." She shook her head. "But these things happen in life, and I know I'm not the only one to lose someone I loved."

"Did it really help to talk about it?" he asked.

"Not to my friends." She pulled her fingers through her dark hair. "I find that when you go through something like that, people shy away. They don't want to hear about it. It's everyone's worst nightmare."

"Yeah, I could see that. So, who did you talk to?"

"My church had a support group of widows. Most of them were elderly ladies, but they fully understood what I was going through, and that was the place where I was able to really talk it through." Rachel looked over at him thoughtfully. "I'm sure the fire station has therapists for you guys."

He nodded slowly. "And I recommend them to all my firefighters."

"But you don't use the services," she concluded.

"No."

"Why not?"

He raised an eyebrow, then shrugged. "I don't need it."

Her laughter bubbled up, soft and lightly amused. "Everyone needs to talk, Matt."

"Maybe so, but not everyone needs therapy."

He knew his aversion to therapy was rooted in his male pride, but he couldn't bring himself to call up a phone line and have some twenty-five-year-old with next to no life experience ask him, *And how does that make you feel?* He could do that himself. He was well aware how he felt. He felt responsible for a little girl's death. He felt sad for everything she would miss, sad for her parents who would never be the same without her. He felt angry at God for not stepping in, and irritated with the town for grieving so publicly. People who didn't even know the girl held candles at vigils. People who only saw her picture in a paper waxed poetic about a life lost too soon. It was one big outpouring of public grief—complete strangers never once thinking that their cathartic release might be pure torture for someone else.

"I get it," she said quietly.

"Do you?"

"Some things you need to sort out with a little privacy."

"Exactly," he agreed, eyeing her with mild surprise.

She nodded slowly. "Everyone means well, but no one seems to really understand, do they?"

"You seem to."

A small smile tickled the corners of her lips, and a soft blush rose in her cheeks. "I came to Haggerston to give my son a new start…" She pressed her lips together and shot him an uncertain look. "Is it terrible that I'm glad to get away from the sympathy?"

"You don't like people to give their condolences?" he asked.

"I sound heartless, don't I?" She shook her head. "I just prefer some privacy when I deal with personal things."

He chuckled softly. "We're more alike than I thought."

"We are." Her eyes crinkled into a smile.

Matt's phone blipped, the signal for an incoming

email. He slid his finger across the screen, and the email popped up.

Mr. Bailey,
It was a pleasure to meet you the other day, and I'm recommending that you go further in the interview process. The next step will include an evaluation by myself, or another member of the hiring committee. I will be in touch about the details soon.
Good luck and all the best,
Abe Bernard

Matt slipped his phone into his pocket. This job as fire chief in South Maitland wasn't guaranteed, but it would be a welcome escape from Haggerston's barrage of memories. Didn't they say that a change was as good as a rest? A step up in his career, and a step outside the town that held his biggest regret seemed like the answer—at least to him. He glanced over at Rachel to find her eyeing him curiously.

"Just a work email," he said, and she nodded. "I should get going, actually."

"Sure." She rose to her feet, and as he stood up next to her, he realized that some of the tension he'd been carrying around the past few weeks had seeped away.

"Thanks," he said. "Are we still on for Friday—that talk at the church?"

"Of course." She smiled. "Just tell me how much advice you want. I don't want to overdo it."

"I can take it." He chuckled.

"Mom!" Chris called from a church window. "Do you see me?"

Her attention moved away from him to the little boy

hanging out a basement window. She moved toward the church, laughing at her son's antics, then glanced back at Matt.

"See you Friday!" she called over her shoulder.

Matt waved and turned back toward his truck. He looked up at the church as he passed, the wind-blasted wood, the gravestones, the oldest of which were tipping dangerously, and the expanse of field beyond. Rachel wasn't responsible for the Montana scenery, but it certainly felt different with her standing in the middle of it all.

Chapter Six

Friday evening, Rachel stood in the kitchen with a mug of coffee in one hand and a muffin in the other. She'd already called Christopher to come down nearly an hour ago so he could eat something before Aunt Louise arrived, and he'd mumbled something about not being hungry, which she didn't entirely believe. He generally chose play over mealtime—especially when dinner was something he didn't like, such as beef stew—which left Rachel now standing in the kitchen, wondering what she could leave for him to eat while she was gone. He wouldn't eat the stew she'd made. She grabbed her son's favorite box of cereal and deposited it in the center of the table with a bowl and a spoon.

"If he doesn't want to eat at mealtime, I should let him get his own cereal," she muttered to herself. She spoiled him, and she knew it, always doing everything for him instead of making him do it for himself. In a concession with the other side of her brain, she left the milk in the fridge for him to fetch on his own.

"That will teach him—" Something. Self-reliance? An appreciation for refrigerated dairy products? Who was she kidding? She'd leave Louise money to order pizza anyway. This was mostly bravado—a warning about what happened when a boy didn't listen to his mom about mealtimes.

This was most definitely a power struggle, and now wasn't the time for power struggles. She hoped her aunt was right, and the birthday party would make a difference—give him a sense of belonging with this mishmash of Emmetts.

She took another bite of muffin and chewed thoughtfully, letting the crumbs fall into the sink. The kitchen was already taking on a new feel from when they first moved in. The scent of her grandmother's house was dissipating, being replaced by the nonsmell of her own stuff. She knew she must have a scent, too—one that would be identified by her own grandchildren, hopefully without a wrinkled nose. The old childhood memories of this room were fading, turning cloudy and thin, where a few weeks ago they'd stood as solid as real people, sitting on kitchen chairs and using up the counter space. She was slowly, unintentionally creating her own memories here and cluttering up her grandmother's kitchen with her own dishes, fridge magnets and boxes of still-packed china.

The front door opened and Aunt Louise called out a cheery "I'm here! Hello, hello!"

Rachel swallowed her last bite of muffin before calling a dry "In here!"

Aunt Louise came through to the kitchen. She smiled brightly and looked around. "It's coming together, isn't it?"

"It seems to be." Rachel smiled back. "How are you?"

"Not too bad. I can't complain." Aunt Louise always

said the same thing, whether the earth was caving in or not. "Did you know Uncle Herman?"

"No... Wait. I think I met him once when I visited Grandma. Does he own a cherry orchard, by any chance?"

"That's him. He passed away."

"What?" Rachel felt an unbidden wave of sadness at this news.

"Yes, it was quite sudden. A stroke."

"Will there be a funeral?"

"No, no. He was a private sort. He'll be cremated, they say, and his son will take his remains back to South Dakota."

"Oh." Rachel frowned. "I'm really sorry. That's awful. Were you close?"

"He was my cousin. We grew up together."

"I didn't really know him well," Rachel admitted. "But I still should have called him or something. I meant to."

"Time gets away from us," Louise replied sympathetically. "The phone works both ways, you know."

Rachel felt the smile tug at the corners of her lips. "You are very pragmatic, Auntie."

"There's no virtue in carrying around a load of guilt" came the reply.

"I'd meant to bring Chris to that orchard, and I'd forgotten who owned it," she said. "I can't seem to re-create it all for him."

"Re-create what?"

"Grandma's house, the lazy summer days, that feeling of being part of a big family..." She took a sip of coffee.

"And you won't be able to. Grandma's gone. Time marches on. It's not your childhood anymore, dear."

"He needs something, and I'd hoped Haggerston would be the right thing for him."

"This is a fine town, but it's going to be something different for him. He'll remember you, not Grandma. He'll remember his own little adventures and lessons. He'll never know your mom and dad, God rest their souls, and he'll never know Uncle Herman."

"Which is sad."

"It's very sad that he won't know your parents, but he's not missing too much with Herman," Louise retorted. "Herman had gotten quite rude in his declining years. He spent most days screaming at the TV. He hated politicians. I kept away, too."

"Oh." Rachel chuckled softly. "He seemed nicer when I met him."

"That was twenty years ago, dear. A lot of things change in twenty years—including my waistline, might I add?"

Rachel rolled her eyes, then called up at the ceiling, "Chris, Aunt Louise is here! Come down and say hi!"

There was no answer, and Rachel sighed.

"So, what are your plans for tonight?" Louise asked, nonplussed by her great-nephew's lack of manners.

"Matt is doing a fire-safety presentation at a local church, so I'm going along to see him in action and give him a few tips."

"Ah." Louise grinned. "A good reason to get together."

"Oh, stop that." Rachel laughed. "This is professional."

"Entirely." Louise nodded sagely, but a smile still tickled the corners of her lips.

Rachel grabbed some bread and popped it into the

toaster, and she was about to holler up the stairs once more when she smelled the acrid scent of smoke coming from somewhere outside.

"Do you smell that?" Rachel asked. She heaved open the kitchen window and craned her neck to see past the lilac bush, just far enough to make out a belch of black smoke.

"What on earth?" she muttered and hurried to the back door to get a better look. Standing on the steps, she was met with a sight that chilled her blood. Chris stood next to a metal trash can, flames leaping out of it. They shot straight up into the air, high enough to tickle the eaves with smoky tongues of flame. The boy seemed frozen, staring up at the blaze in mute horror. Her stomach dropped. She'd thought he was still upstairs—how did she miss this?

"Chris!" she shouted. "Chris! Get back!" Turning back to her aunt, she barked, "Call 911!"

Rachel dashed forward, and inside the house the fire alarm went off in a piercing whistle. She grabbed Chris by the shoulder and pulled him farther from the blaze, then looked around impotently for something to squelch the flames.

Oh, God, help me!

Rachel's eyes lit upon a roll of old carpet sticking out from the garbage pile waiting to be picked up later that week. She ran for the carpet and pulled it jerkily from the heap. Limbs, trimmed from nearby trees, fell away from the pile, scattering around the grass as Rachel dragged the carpet toward the trash can. She wasn't sure what she intended to do with the massive roll— beat the fire or smother it being her first instincts—

but she couldn't get past the blistering heat. She simply stood with the roll in her quivering arms, staring at the flames as they stretched closer to the wooden siding of the house, flames leaping across the divide.

I'm going to lose this old house, she thought in one moment of dismal clarity. *I'm going to lose it all.*

As Matt's truck cruised down Rachel's street, he was mentally going over the presentation for the youth group. Maybe it was male pride, but he wanted Rachel to see him at his best tonight, and as much as he argued with himself otherwise, it wasn't only about the job. Her words from their talk in the graveyard had been going through his mind the past couple of days—more accurately, *she* had been going through his mind, and he hadn't been able to chase her out.

Golden evening sunshine slanted down from a bright, cloudless sky. A gentle breeze rustled through the leaves of the trees lining the street. It was a perfect day, except for the scent of smoke hanging in the air. Matt glanced around, slowing his vehicle. He wondered if someone was burning some brush in their backyard, but the closer he came to Rachel's home, he made out the piercing beeps of a fire alarm growing louder.

"That's no bonfire," Matt muttered, and he picked up his radio and pushed down the button.

"This is Deputy Chief Bailey. We've got a fire on Elm Street—visible smoke and fire alarm going off. We need a unit down here ASAP."

He didn't wait for an answer, but dropped the handset back into its holder and slammed on the brakes in front of Rachel's home. Smoke billowed from behind the house, wafting over the roof in an ominous, acrid cloud. The fire alarm was shrieking from an open window, and a dog next door was barking in frantic response. Without another thought, Matt reached behind his seat and hoisted out a large fire extinguisher, his muscles straining with the weight of the cylinder and the awkward reach. Heaving it free, he kicked open his door and jogged around the side of the house toward the source of the belching smoke.

Roaring flames were leaping up out of a garbage can. Rachel stood by, a roll of carpet on one shoulder, her eyes red with smoke and an expression of horror on her face. The orange tongues licked at the side of the house, a black scorch mark growing ever larger.

"Rachel!" Matt shouted, and she turned her wide eyes toward him. It took a moment for her to register him; then she snapped out of her frozen state. She took a step back and planted a hand in the middle of her son's chest, pressing him back, too. Louise stood behind them, a cordless phone in one hand.

Matt pointed the hose toward the base of the fire and pressed the lever to release the pounding flow of foam. The cylinder trembled in his hands from the sheer force of the pressure, and he walked closer, shooting the contents of the fire extinguisher straight into the garbage can, then up the side of the house to squelch the last of the licking flames.

A siren wailed up the street and a fire truck eased to a stop in front of the house. The familiar sound of boots hitting pavement registered in the back of his mind, but his gaze was fixed on Rachel. She stood in the same position, her hand on her son's chest, and her red-rimmed eyes welled with tears. She dropped her arm and wiped her cheeks with the flats of her palms.

"You okay?" He angled his steps around the charred garbage can.

She nodded and sucked in a deep breath. "Thank you."

For a moment, Matt considered his professional reserve, but there was something about those dewy eyes that forced it from his mind. He stepped forward, put his arms around her and pulled her against his chest. She didn't resist, and she leaned her cheek against his shirt, the dampness of her tears seeping through the fabric and pressing against his skin. He rested his chin on the top of her warm head and smoothed down her tangled hair.

"Are you okay, kiddo?" he asked Chris.

Rachel pulled away from Matt's embrace and she dropped to her knees in front of the boy, just as the firefighters came into the backyard. They tramped across the grass in full gear, their movement heavy and strong.

"Hey, DC, everything under control?" Firefighter Johnson asked, his headgear under one arm.

"Yeah, it was pretty well contained. Took one fire extinguisher. It looked worse from the front of the house."

"It's a good thing you were here" came the reply. The big man eyed the scorched side of the house. "Could have been worse."

"True enough." Matt nodded. "I'll take care of the rest. You guys can head back."

Johnson nodded and beckoned the others back toward the truck, but he did cast one curious glance toward Rachel, a smile flickering at the corners of his lips. Matt caught Johnson's gaze and held it, raising one eyebrow questioningly. Red suffused the man's face and he headed back around the house toward the truck, and this time, he didn't look back.

Matt turned back toward Rachel. She was squatting next to her son, and the boy was looking resolutely away from her, fighting tears.

"Everything okay?" Matt asked quietly, hunkering down onto a step next to Chris.

"I'll give you some space," Louise said, her voice shaky. "My goodness... Thank God you were here, Mr. Bailey." Her words trailed off as she headed back into the house, and Matt turned his attention back to the boy beside him.

"I was just asking Chris how the fire started," Rachel said. "Was it already burning when you came outside?"

Chris didn't answer.

"Did you see who started it?"

Still no reply, but Chris's face crumpled.

"Was someone in our yard?" she pressed.

"No, I didn't see anything," Chris wept. "I don't know."

"Oh, Chris..." Rachel wrapped her arms around her son and pulled him close against her. She rocked him back and forth, and when the boy stopped crying, she wiped his eyes.

"Okay," Rachel said, boosting him to his feet. "Chris, I want you to run inside and go wash your face and change your clothes. Everything is fine now. We're safe."

The boy looked back at her cautiously. "Are you mad at me, Mom?"

"No, sweetheart. I was just scared."

As Chris disappeared with a bang of the screen door, Rachel sank down onto the space her son had recently occupied, and she glanced up at Matt. Her creamy skin was streaked with smoke and a smear of dirt.

"We had another fire before we moved. In the backyard," she said.

"You don't think it was so accidental?" Matt asked, arching an eyebrow.

"I wish I knew." She heaved a tired sigh. "Chris is what they call a troubled kid, and I have no idea what to do. I don't want to blame him for something he didn't do, either."

Matt's gaze moved around the yard. A bike leaned against a scrawny apple tree, and a couple of yellow tractors sat in the middle of a flower bed. A roll of carpet lay, awkwardly bent in the center, by the blackened garbage can, and he frowned.

"What were you going to do with that carpet?" he asked.

Soft laughter bubbled up inside her. "I don't know. I think I wanted to hit the fire with it."

Matt shot her a grin. "That's pretty heavy. If you'd been twice as big, it might have worked."

"If you hadn't arrived when you did, I might have had to give it a try," she retorted.

"You think on your feet." He eyed her, impressed. She might be petite and appear to be as fragile as a teacup, but she had strength under there.

"Thanks."

Matt shot Rachel a sympathetic smile.

"Normally, people start fires for profit—you know, insurance money, that sort of thing—but when kids do it, it's because they're mad and they don't have any other outlet."

"If he is, it's my fault."

"If he is that angry, it's resolvable," he countered. "You can figure it out. I have the business cards of some family therapists, if you're interested."

"Thanks." She smiled wanly. "I'm not sure what I want to do yet, but I appreciate it."

"Tough day, huh?" he said. "I guess you'll want to stay home tonight."

"No, I want to go," she said.

"You sure?" He didn't want to pressure her, take her away from her son when he needed her most.

"Yes, I'm sure." She pushed herself to her feet. "I'll bring Chris with me, though. He could use a little fire-safety talk, and I think I could use the comfort of some church."

She wiped at her cheeks one last time, smearing the dirt again. She had no idea how ruffled or endearing she looked right now, and for the life of him, he wished that he could comfort her. But before he could try, she pushed herself to her feet.

"Come on in. I won't be too long," she said, sucking in a shaky breath.

He had nothing left to do but follow her into the house.

The Haggerston Christian Assembly was located in the downtown core of the town. It was a newer building, cheerful brick with a white steeple and cross rising up from a sloping roof. A church sign announced Fire Safety for the Community. Everyone Welcome. As they stepped into the foyer, Rachel steered Chris over to the side and bent down to his level.

"How are you doing?" she asked quietly.

"Okay."

"That fire was pretty scary, wasn't it?"

"But Mr. Bailey put it out."

"Yes, he did." She brushed a wisp of his hair of his forehead. "And God took care of us, too."

Chris nodded. "Are you sure you aren't mad?"

"Is there a reason I should be?" she asked carefully.

"No."

"I'm not mad, Chris. I was really scared. I didn't want anything to happen to you, and I didn't want our new home to burn down."

"Okay."

"I love you, honey," she said softly. "More than anything in the whole world. Do you know that?"

"Yeah."

"Good." She kissed his forehead. "I know we hadn't planned for you to come with me, but are you going to sit quietly for me while we listen to Mr. Bailey's presentation?"

He nodded. While she wanted to believe otherwise, the unpleasant suspicion that her son had started the fire nagged at the back of her mind, and she pushed it aside. There was time enough to sort it out later, and he wasn't in any present danger, thanks to Matt's timely arrival.

"Let's go in and sit down," Matt suggested. "After the song service, I'm up."

The back was blessedly empty, and they slid onto the polished pew. Matt's knee jiggled and when she glanced at him, he stopped the movement and gave her an apologetic shrug. He glanced around the sanctuary, and for the first time Rachel realized that he wasn't comfortable here—and she was pretty sure it wasn't anxiety over a presentation.

"You aren't much of a churchgoer, are you?" she whispered.

"Not lately."

She nodded. Faith and church were personal, and she didn't want to pry into more than he was willing to share. They sat together as the preliminaries were taken care of—welcoming members of the community for this fire-safety seminar and making a few announcements about an upcoming wedding shower. Chris grabbed a pencil and a tithe envelope from the back of the pew, and she knew that he wanted to draw, but she tapped his knee and shook her head.

"Pay attention," she whispered. "I want you to listen."

When Matt's time came, he rose to his feet and headed toward the front of the church. Rachel put her arm across the back of the pew behind her son. Matt accepted the mic from the man who had announced him, and his gaze moved over the audience, settling on Rachel. He smiled ever so slightly, and she found herself smiling back. Matt's voice echoed warmly around the church as he began his talk, and she settled into the back pew once more. He was eloquent and personable, but she could see why he had trouble speaking with smaller children—teenagers were his perfect audience. The teenagers were enthralled with his stories and looked generally in awe of him. She couldn't blame them. He spoke about the dangers of fire, how he prayed before dashing into each smoking building and how sad he was because most of those fires had been preventable. From there, he moved into some simple ways to protect homes and buildings from the risk of fire. She was impressed.

The talk went well, and when it was over, they filed

YOUR PARTICIPATION IS REQUESTED!

Dear Reader,

Since you are a lover of our books – we would like to get to know you!

Inside you will find a short Reader's Survey. Sharing your answers with us will help our editorial staff understand who you are and what activities you enjoy.

To thank you for your participation, we would like to send you 2 books and 2 gifts – **ABSOLUTELY FREE!**

Enjoy your gifts with our appreciation,

Pam Powers

**SEE INSIDE
FOR READER'S
SURVEY**

For Your Reading Pleasure...

We'll send you 2 books and 2 gifts
ABSOLUTELY FREE
just for completing our Reader's Survey!

out and Rachel and Chris met up with Matt in the foyer. He raised his eyebrows questioningly.

"So?" he asked quietly. "How was I?"

"Excellent." She shook her head. "You're a wonderful public speaker."

"Thanks, but I need some tips…"

"You don't need any for an older age group," she said. "You had their attention the entire time, but I can see why younger kids are a challenge. Your natural presentation style is better suited to an older audience."

"See?" He grinned. "This is what I need to hear."

"With smaller children, your anecdotes would have to be much shorter—and less intense, of course." She paused as Chris came up beside her. She looked down at her son. "Did you learn anything?"

"Yeah." He nodded. "I want to be a firefighter when I grow up."

Rachel smiled, then faltered. Had she achieved her goal here? She wasn't sure.

"Let's head out," Matt said, putting a hand in the small of her back and guiding them toward the door.

Someone tapped her arm and she turned to see a woman in her forties. She wore a floral dress and had her graying hair cropped short.

"May I speak with you a moment?" the woman asked quietly.

Rachel nodded and hung back. Matt and Chris carried on toward the front door, Matt pausing to speak with a few people on the way. Rachel smiled uncertainly.

The woman opened one hand, revealing a pack of matches. Rachel reached out tentatively and picked them up.

Alphonzo's Pizza.

"Where did you get these?" Rachel asked.

"Your son accidentally dropped them." She smiled gently. "Mom to mom, I thought you might want to know."

"Thanks."

Rachel opened the pack to find only two matches remaining. Her stomach sank and tears pricked her eyes. It looked like the confirmation she'd been so afraid of.

"I'm Wendy Martin, by the way," the woman said with a gentle smile.

"I'm Rachel Carter. Nice to meet you." Rachel blinked back the mist of tears. "I'm sorry, I don't mean to be so emotional. It's been one of those days."

"Don't I know about that?" Wendy squeezed her hand sympathetically. "Hang in there. Parenting isn't for the faint of heart."

Sometimes it took another mother to understand these things. She glanced in Matt's direction. He stood at the front door of the church, said goodbye to a young family and turned toward her. He smiled at her, but when his gaze landed on Wendy, he froze for an instant, and he pasted on a professional smile. Rachel could recognize the difference.

"Hello," Wendy said quietly as they walked up, and she and Matt exchanged an unfathomable look.

"Mrs. Martin." Matt cleared his throat. "It's nice to see you."

Wendy put her hand out to shake his but got no response, so let her hand drop, just as Matt responded to her initial gesture a beat too late. She laughed uncomfortably and put her hand out again and they shook awkwardly.

"It's nice to see you, too," she said. "In church, I mean." She cleared her throat. "It's nice."

"I'm afraid you just caught us on our way out," Matt said.

"Oh, of course." Wendy nodded quickly and took a step back. "Well, take care."

"You, too."

Matt's gaze swept over them, any earlier intimacy sealed away behind that professional veneer. He reached out and put a warm hand on Rachel's arm, but when she looked up at him questioningly, she couldn't get past that grim reserve.

As they stepped outside, she voiced her confusion.

"What happened in there?" she asked.

"What do you mean?"

"Wendy Martin—is she related to Natalie?"

Matt didn't answer, and they walked toward his truck in silence.

"Who is Natalie?" Chris piped in curiously.

"Never mind, honey," she said quickly. She'd explain later, as best she could, but this wasn't a conversation to have in front of Matt. He was most certainly not past the pain of that fire, but she didn't understand the tension between him and Wendy Martin—unless she was the mother.

Matt opened the back door to his pickup and Chris hopped inside. He slammed it shut, then turned to Rachel, his eyes clouded with dark emotions.

"Things get complicated in a place this size," he said, his voice low. "Really complicated."

"Is she Natalie's mom?" Rachel asked.

"Yeah. You know how you talk about how a fresh start is the answer?"

Rachel nodded mutely.

"Well, I need this job in South Maitland. Badly."

He opened her door and gave her a hand up into the cab. When she was seated, he slammed it shut before heading around to the other side. She looked out the window to see Wendy Martin standing with a group of people in front of the church, but she was looking toward Matt's truck, an unreadable expression on her face.

Natalie's mother.

Rachel couldn't imagine the kind of pain that woman had endured losing her daughter. She couldn't fully appreciate the pain Matt faced in not being able to save the child. She looked down at the pack of matches in her hand, her own parental misgivings rising up inside her.

Matt paused outside the truck to talk briefly with a man, and Rachel took the opportunity to talk to her son.

"Chris," she said, turning around. "Are these yours?"

She held out the matches, and Chris blanched.

"Are they?" she pressed.

He nodded.

"And did you start that fire today?" She kept her voice gentle and low.

Chris nodded, his lips quivering. "I didn't mean for it to get that big."

"I believe you," she said quietly. "I wish you would have told me the truth before."

"I couldn't. Not with Mr. Bailey there."

She nodded, a lump rising in her throat. Confession wasn't easy, and she'd put him on the spot with an audience. "But you know not to ever do that again, don't you?"

"I won't," he whispered. "Not ever. I promise."

She reached back and took his hand, and then Matt

pulled open the driver's side door. This situation was so much bigger than she knew how to handle. What they all needed right now was God's guidance.

Chapter Seven

The next afternoon, Rachel frowned at her computer screen, tabbing down a list of articles. An untouched plate of watermelon sat beside her, and a breeze whisked through the window, stirring the hair that lay on her moist forehead. The smell of smoke still lingered in the air from the day before.

"Hello!" Aunt Louise sang out, knocking at the front door. "Anybody home?"

"In the kitchen!" Rachel called back, not stirring from her spot. The screen door banged and her aunt appeared around the corner, a bag of fresh corn on the cob in one hand.

"I brought some corn for the birthday party," Aunt Louise said, depositing her gift on the kitchen table. She looked over Rachel's shoulder at the laptop screen. "What're you doing?"

"I'm trying to figure something out," Rachel replied, shooting her aunt a smile. "And I think I need your help."

Aunt Louise looked down at Rachel's laptop in interest, pulling up a chair. "I'll do what I can."

"Three years ago, there was a school fire here in town," Rachel said.

"Yes, of course. That poor little girl died. It was awful."

Rachel nodded. "What do you remember about that?"

"Why the sudden interest?" Aunt Louise asked. "You aren't reconsidering your job at the school, are you?"

"No, no," Rachel replied with a shake of her head. "It's hard to explain, but I need to know more."

"Because of Matt Bailey."

Heat rose in her cheeks. "Sort of."

Louise shot her an amused look. "I don't see any other reason why you'd be so interested in all the minor details."

"I suppose this is about Matt. I just don't understand it. He's very private, and I know about the fire, but I also saw something at the church yesterday."

"What?" The older woman leaned forward.

"Weird tension," she replied. "And since I can't figure out what to do with my son at the moment, I've decided to try to figure this out instead."

Upstairs, Chris's voice, singing his own version of "She'll Be Coming Round the Mountain," rang out, and both women looked upward.

"Did he set the fire?" Louise asked, her voice low.

"Yes."

"On purpose?"

Rachel shook her head. "He's seven. I don't think he fully understood the consequences of a lit match."

"You know that saying, sometimes a cigar is just a cigar?" Louise asked.

"Sometimes a fire is just a fire?" Rachel sighed.

"Sometimes a child's mistake is just a mistake and

not a sign of impending doom. I seem to remember you launching yourself out a window with a plastic shopping bag for a parachute, and you weren't suicidal."

"No, but I broke my ankle."

Her aunt nodded. "That you did. Your mom told me that you were the most popular kid in school that September. It didn't end your life. I know this is serious, but be careful how you handle it. Kids are like self-fulfilling prophecies. If you treat them like delinquents, they tend to meet expectations."

Overhead, Chris plowed into the second verse of the song, and Rachel nodded. Even if there were bigger issues at play, he was happy and playing for the time being.

"You're right, Auntie," she said.

"Good, now on to this handsome firefighter of yours," Louise said with a smile. "What do you want to know?"

"What happened?" Rachel asked.

"There was a fire." Louise sighed. "They say a parent started it. His wife left him and she got full custody of the kids. He wanted his family back, but he had some large emotional problems. He set the fire and thought he would swoop in and save his kids and prove something to them, or their mother. The school went up in flames and almost all the kids got out, except for Natalie. They couldn't account for her. Matthew Bailey went once more after the rest had given up, and by the time he brought her out—" Louise stopped.

None of this was new information, and it didn't explain what she'd seen. She was silent for a moment; then she asked, "How did the community react?"

"In grief, of course." Louise picked up a piece of watermelon, then put it back on the plate without tasting it. "There were vigils in her honor, a plaque was put up at the school in her memory…" She frowned. "Last year, City Hall held a memorial day for the fire and collected donations to be given to a children's charity in Natalie Martin's name."

"It sounds like they meant well," Rachel said softly. "What about the family?"

"The mother was in the news at first, very tearful and heartbroken. She had other children to care for, though, and eventually the family asked for some privacy from the papers and local TV channels. Everyone respected that."

Rachel pushed back her computer and sat in thoughtful silence for a moment. She could understand that desire to grieve alone, but something was missing in her mental picture of the tragedy.

"What about Matt?" she asked.

"What about him?"

"Was he ever mentioned in these tributes?"

"From time to time. He was the heroic firefighter who did his best."

"A public memorial to his most crushing failure," Rachel concluded.

Louise paused, then winced. "I don't think anyone meant it that way."

"No, of course not." She smiled sadly. "No one knows how to do these things. Grief is awkward and ugly. Memorials and tributes help to clean it up a little."

Her aunt nodded sympathetically. "You understand him, don't you?"

Rachel glanced over in mild surprise. "I suppose I do, in a way."

"Is he—" Louise looked to the side, then sighed. "Does the fire—"

The fire followed him, as did the memory of little Natalie, that much Rachel knew for a fact, but she also knew that he was too private to share that with just anyone. He shouldered his grief alone, and by some happenstance, he'd shared a small piece of it with her. She couldn't betray his confidence.

"I don't think it's the sort of thing that a man just forgets," Rachel replied. "But I couldn't speak for him."

"No, of course not," Louise agreed.

Rachel clicked on a news photo of the previous year's memorial on her computer. The mayor held a large check for a children's hospital charity, given in Natalie Martin's name. In the background, Matt Bailey stood rigid and professional. His uniform was crisp and the buttons gleamed. His hat sat perfectly straight across his forehead, and his expression was as blank as a palace guard's, but something in his eyes gave her pause.

Agony. His eyes betrayed the emotions battling inside him, the emotions no one else noticed in that brief moment, captured by camera.

If it isn't this job, it will be another one, she realized. *He's leaving this town one way or another.*

And she couldn't say that she blamed him.

Matt straightened his back and pushed the report across his desk. It had been a long morning of paperwork—prefire safety reports, employee fitness reviews and all the sundry running of a town fire department.

There was a tap on the door and Firefighter Johnson poked his head into the office.

"DC, we're heading out to get some lunch. Interested?"

"I'm good," Matt replied with a wave of his hand. "Thanks, though."

"Oh, we came across this…" The man tossed an envelope onto Matt's desk and Matt gave a distracted nod in thanks, shoving the envelope to the top of his inbox.

The door shut again, and Matt turned his attention back to the report. The words swam before his eyes and he rubbed his hands over his face. His arms and chest still burned from his morning workout—admittedly, a more intense workout than he normally did on a Monday morning. The weight room in the fire station always had at least one guy in it, lifting weights or running on the treadmill, but this morning Matt had had the machines to himself, which was just as well. He had a lot of frustration to purge from his system, and that kind of workout was most effective without an audience.

"What was I even thinking yesterday?" he muttered to himself.

He'd stayed away from church to avoid those awkward encounters like the one he'd had with Wendy Martin. He could deal with some discomfort, and he could recover from hard memories, but his biggest irritation was having Rachel front row center to see it all—that audience he so resented. It was more than that, though. Rachel was different. She wasn't a firefighter whose respect he needed to retain. She was… He sighed.

Don't go there, he reminded himself. *No use starting something you can't finish.*

His desk phone rang, and Matt picked up the receiver, grateful for some distraction.

"Deputy Chief Bailey," he said.

"Hi, this is Abe Bernard. How are you?"

"Can't complain." Matt's mind refocused and he pulled a hand through his hair. "What can I do for you?"

"I'm coming through Haggerston on Friday, and I was hoping to shadow you for a few hours and see you in action."

"This is the observation that you emailed about, isn't it?" Matt asked with a smile.

"Yes, sir, it is." Mr. Bernard agreed. "We are very impressed with you. This will be the last stage before we make a decision."

Matt leaned across his desk to check the calendar and inwardly groaned. He'd be addressing a day camp full of kids that day. He'd decided to do the presentation himself so that Rachel could give him some tips with a younger group, but it looked as though time had run out.

"I could probably shift my schedule around a bit—" Matt began.

"If you need to, but I won't need any babysitting," the other man said. "I'll just be there to observe. I'll need to see you in a managerial capacity, but before this process is done, I'll also want to see how you are with community groups."

"You might get both on Friday," Matt admitted grudgingly. "I'm going to be addressing a kids' day camp about fire safety."

"Excellent," Mr. Bernard crowed. "That would certainly speed things along for me. Do you have any questions at all?"

"I do," Matt said. "How many candidates are there for this position?"

"Four, but I have to admit, you're standing out from the group. You've got the experience, the recommendations and the education."

"That's good to hear," Matt said, satisfaction flooding over him. Hopefully, his standing wouldn't change after Mr. Bernard saw him with a school group.

"I'll see you on Friday, Matt. Take care."

As he hung up the phone, Matt nodded to himself. He'd worked hard toward a fire chief position for years. He was young, he knew. Most men put in a lot more time before they qualified for the position, but then he wasn't most men.

Lord, I've been working toward this since the beginning, he prayed silently. *I want this.*

Matt turned back to the paperwork, but his eye moved to the envelope on the top of papers. He paused for a moment, then reached over and picked it up. He slid a finger under the flap to tear the seal and looked inside to find a single Polaroid picture. Before he pulled it out, he knew what it was—a grainy photo of Matt sitting in one of the firehouse armchairs, a newborn in his arms. He looked awkward, the sleeping baby being the more comfortable of the two of them. With one hand he supported the infant's diapered rump, and with the other he held an empty baby bottle aloft. Written in ballpoint pen across the bottom were the words *Bailey's Baby*.

That was how everyone had referred to Christopher that night, and Matt recalled being mildly annoyed at the playful picture taking. Normally at that time of night they'd all be turned in for sleep in the bunks, but the hours stretched out in sleepless baby duties. All Christopher seemed to want to do was drink bottle after bottle and sleep in Matt's arms.

Secretly, under the gruff exterior, Matt had been proud that the baby preferred him, and when he handed the sleeping infant to the social worker, he'd felt a pang of loss.

Without ever meaning to, he'd bonded with the kid.

"I forgot we took this," he murmured to himself, running his thumb over the thick edge of the photo. He moved to put it down, but then he changed his mind and tucked it into his front shirt pocket.

Glancing at his watch, he logged out of his computer and grabbed his hat. He had an appointment for a pre-fire inspection at Doug's Bakery. Doug wanted to renovate his kitchen, but he had to be sure he wouldn't be breaking any fire codes in the process. Matt couldn't really complain. Doug was not only the source of the best doughnuts in town; he was also Matt's second cousin. Matt needed this distraction. Work was better than overthinking the things he couldn't change.

Rachel scanned the bakery display case, filled with a mouthwatering array of chocolate-dipped cream puffs, sugar-powdered doughnuts and flaky turnovers. Just the aroma probably carried calories, and Rachel stared down at the options, attempting to exert some self-control. The sweet scent of baking wafted through the small shop. One whole wall was dedicated to a variety of freshly baked breads and bagels, and a platter of bread samples sat just out of her reach next to a little dish of butter. She eyed them hungrily.

"Can I help you, miss?" a teenage boy asked. He wore a white smock and a hair net—not a flattering look for the young man, but his smile was easy and his stance carefree.

"Yes, I'd like to order a birthday cake," she replied,

tearing her eyes from the cubes of rye bread and forcing herself back to the task at hand.

The young man pulled out a binder of cake options, and she flipped through glossy photos of everything from wedding cakes to cupcakes.

"I just need a simple sheet cake," she said. "Like this." She pointed to an example in the binder.

"Do you want white cake, lemon cake or chocolate?" the young man asked.

"Let's do white cake with chocolate icing," Rachel said.

"I'd recommend the buttercream icing. We can do that in chocolate."

"That sounds delicious. And on the top, could you write—"

Rachel took the slip of paper the young man offered her and wrote the message for the top of the cake. Out of the corner of her eye, she caught the door to the kitchen opening, and a thin man with small wire glasses came out, a baker's hat tucked under one arm.

"So you think there's room for another oven?" the man asked someone behind him.

"As long as you leave those twenty-four inches before that door, you'll be fine. But measure carefully, if you want to stay within fire regulations."

Rachel glanced up, recognizing Matt's voice immediately. He seemed to notice her at the same moment, and their eyes met in mutual surprise. Matt's dark blue shirt was open at the neck, his blue eyes meeting hers from under the rim of his formal hat. A smile teased the corners of his lips.

"Hi," Matt said.

The smaller man looked from Matt to Rachel, curiosity written on his face. He wore the bakery smock as well, and he carried himself with quick, efficient movements.

"Doug, this is Rachel Carter. She's new in town. Rachel, this is Doug, the owner of this bakery."

"And his cousin," Doug added with a grin.

"And my cousin."

"Nice to meet you." Rachel smiled and shook the man's hand. "I was just ordering a cake."

"Special occasion?" Matt sauntered around the display case to her side. She inwardly winced. Had he noticed that he hadn't been invited?

Matt leaned against the counter, his strong, warm arm brushing hers. As he glanced down at the paper in front of her, the musky scent of his cologne tugged at her, and she stoically ignored it.

"Chris turned seven last month, but since we were getting ready to move, I thought we'd take another swing at a birthday cake tomorrow. The first one was a home-made disaster."

"Doug's cakes are great. You'll start celebrating Tuesdays as an excuse to have one."

Rachel smiled. "I have no doubt."

Rachel turned back to complete her order. She needed to have the cake ready for that evening, which she was assured wouldn't be a problem. She even had the option of having the cake delivered, which she gratefully accepted. As she finished up with the details, Matt ambled over to the display case and selected a few treats. When they had both paid, Matt angled his head toward the door, a white paper bag in hand.

"Can I walk you out?" he asked, lowering his voice to keep their conversation just between the two of them.

"Sure."

"See you later, Doug," Matt called over his shoulder. Rachel smiled her thanks and followed Matt out the front door, leaving the cool air-conditioning behind them as they sauntered out into the summer heat.

The street wasn't busy this time of day, and Rachel paused to breathe in the scent of begonias from the planters that hung dripping from a fresh watering. Down the street, a pickup truck crept along, a big water container in the back, and a teenage girl leaned out with a sprayer, watering each hanging planter as she passed. Rachel watched the process for a moment, then turned her steps after Matt.

They stopped at a corner and waited for a car to pass before they stepped out into the street and crossed to the other side. Matt paused next to the vehicle and bounced his keys in his palm.

"Look, Matt—" she began. "I'm sorry I didn't invite you to the party."

"It's okay. It's understandable. You need Chris to settle in on his own, with the people who will be part of his life here." He shrugged. "It's okay. I get it."

She sighed. "Okay. I'm glad. If things were different—"

"It's okay," he repeated. "Did you drive?"

"No, I walked," she replied. "I wanted the exercise."

"You seem to do that lot." A smile tickled the corner of his lips.

"It's good for me."

He nodded. "Can't argue with that. Do you want a lift back?"

Rachel considered for a moment, then shrugged. "I do need to get back and get organized for the party."

Matt pulled open the passenger-side door. He handed her up into the seat and deposited the bag of treats into her lap. "Help yourself."

Inside, there was a selection of pastries, and she plucked out an apple turnover and sank her teeth into the flaky pastry, her mouth watering.

"Good?" he asked as he hopped up into the driver's side.

"Hmm." She nodded, chewing.

"Doug's the best, all right." He pulled out a chocolate-covered doughnut and took a bite. Then he started the truck and eased out of the parking spot.

"You don't normally attend church, do you?" she asked.

"Not really."

"Did you used to?"

"Every week."

She nodded. She didn't need the explanation of why he'd stopped. She glanced at him, wondering what he was thinking. His gaze flickered in her direction, and then he signaled for a turn.

"I'm sorry things got weird at the church with Wendy Martin. I didn't mean for you to see that."

"Don't worry about me," she said. "But I think I get it. She's Natalie's mother. What are you supposed to say to her?"

"It's a bit more than that." He stopped at a corner, waiting for a couple of teenagers to cross before he made the turn. "When Natalie died, Wendy was a mess. We all understood that. But she needed someone to blame."

"And she blamed you?" Rachel asked cautiously.

He shrugged. "I was the obvious target. I hadn't gotten her daughter out in time."

The truck rumbled past an auto-body shop and a gardening store on one side of the street, a hardware store on the other. A warm breeze whispered through the open window, and she took another bite of the apple turnover, the flaky pastry melting in her mouth.

"What about the man who started the fire?" she asked. "He seems like a better target to me."

Matt shook his head. "Grief does what it does. It's not always logical."

"You seem to understand that," she said softly. "She doesn't blame you still, does she?"

"No." He popped the last of his cream puff into his mouth. "She and her husband came down to the firehouse and apologized for it. She said she was wrong and after that she became my biggest champion."

"So why the tension?"

Matt was silent for a long moment, and then his big shoulders lifted in a sigh. "Because she was right. It was my fault."

"No." Rachel shook her head adamantly. "How could it have been?"

"Whatever happened in there, it's on my shoulders. I was in charge," Matt went on. "When Wendy decided she didn't blame me after all, it didn't change the facts."

"I read the newspaper articles," Rachel admitted. "Everyone started focusing on the heroic firefighter who'd done his best."

The muscles along Matt's jawline tensed. "Something like that."

"You don't want to be a hero, do you?"

"It isn't about what I want. I'm not a hero," he said, glancing toward her. "A hero would have saved her."

He stopped at a four-way stop and waited as another

car cruised past in front of them. He eased forward again, his broad palm moving over the top of the steering wheel.

"They don't mean to make it harder on you," Rachel said. They were nearing her street.

"I know. I get that." Matt shot her a smile that didn't reach his eyes.

A delivery truck lumbered by and the driver flicked his hat in a salute to Matt, who nodded in return. He shouldered too much responsibility for one man to carry on his own, and sadness welled up inside her at the thought of all he'd been through, all he kept hidden. She'd wanted Chris to bond with family at his party, but she couldn't just leave Matt alone, either. Maybe she'd been a little overprotective—it wouldn't be the first time, and certainly not the last.

"You should come," Rachel said softly.

"Where?" He glanced at her.

"Chris's birthday party."

"Oh…" Matt cleared his throat, then shook his head. "Isn't it better for me to give the kid some space?"

"Sounds like you've had to keep too much personal space lately," she said.

An amused smile tugged at his lips, and then he reached into the bag and pulled out a jelly doughnut. "I'm fine, Rachel. You don't need to rescue me."

He turned onto her street and slowed and parked in front of the house. He was distancing himself from her, and that hurt.

"I'm not rescuing you. I'm inviting you to a birthday party."

"You've asked me to give Chris a little space, and I think that's a good idea. Let's just continue with that."

Rachel nodded, irritation simmering inside her. For a man who didn't want to be called a hero, he sure liked to act as if he could handle everything on his own. Even the toughest person needed someone to lean on—she knew that for a fact.

"I'm not trying to rescue you, Matt," she repeated.

"Aren't you?"

Rachel shook her head. "Are you always like this?"

"Like what?"

"Stubborn."

"Yes. Constantly." He caught her eye and for a brief moment, something tender smoldered in his gaze; then he sighed. "I've got a good chance of getting that job, Rachel."

"Oh…" Her voice sounded breathy in her own ears. "Of course."

"It's probably smart for us to keep things—" He didn't finish the thought.

Keep things professional? Keep things distanced? She knew what he meant—it was what she'd been saying all along, but it felt different coming from him.

He nodded to the bag of treats in her lap. "Keep those."

Rachel opened the door and hopped down, slamming it behind her. The window was still open, and when she looked back, Matt was eyeing her cautiously.

"Matt?"

"Yeah?"

"Thanks for the pastries."

His eyes crinkled up into a smile, and he raised two fingers in a partial wave as he pulled away from the curb.

Rachel stood there for a long moment, looking the way he'd left. The truck rumbled down the street; then he signaled and turned and was out of sight. She heaved a sigh. Maybe she did want to rescue him—a tiny bit. She still felt that it was possible for Matt to be kind to Chris without giving him false hope, but just because it was possible didn't mean it was a tightrope that Matt wanted to walk, and Matt had already made his position more than clear—he was on his way out.

She headed toward the house. She had a party to pull together.

Chapter Eight

"Come on, Matt," Doug urged. "Do me this favor."

"Why can't you drop the cake off yourself?" Matt changed his cell phone to the other ear and glanced at his watch. It was already nearly five, and he was about to leave the firehouse for the day.

"I got a huge order for a funeral tomorrow. Their caterer fell through, and I promised that I'd make up the difference. You know where she lives, right?"

"This is a bit complicated, Doug."

"I noticed that." Doug chortled good-naturedly. "I thought you might thank me for the excuse to go see her."

"I'm trying to keep things professional," Matt replied. He leaned over and logged out of his computer.

"Why?" Doug retorted. "It's high time you found someone, Matt."

Matt shook his head. What was it with every person in the family wanting to get him into a long-term relationship? Besides, he had the kids' day camp presentation the next day, and he needed to brush up on his notes. He reached for the papers Rachel had given him about working with school groups, but they weren't on his desk. Then he remembered where he'd left them—at Rachel's place. He grimaced.

"Fine, fine." At least he'd get his papers at the same time. "I'll drop it by for you. But you owe me one."

Hanging up the phone, Matt dropped a couple of files into a file cabinet and headed for the door. If he was trying to keep things professional with Rachel, this was not the way to do it, but what could he do? His one consolation was that if all went well, in a couple of months he'd be far enough away from his well-meaning family that they wouldn't be able to pester and pressure without a long-distance phone call.

Twenty minutes later, Matt found himself with a boxed cake on the passenger seat, parked in front of Rachel's house. Summer evening sunlight slanted through the trees, casting long shadows across the lawn. The screen door was propped open with an old brick, and the sound of voices and laughter filtered out onto the street. The party appeared to be in full swing.

Matt hopped out of his truck and came around the other side to retrieve the large cake box, then headed toward the front door. His shoes clunked against the wooden stairs, and he poked his head in the front door.

"Hello!" he called.

Several seniors sat around the living room, and they looked up in interest.

"Is that you, Matthew Bailey?" an old woman asked. She had short, permed white hair and wore a crocheted sweater that reminded him of a doily.

"Hi, Mrs. Geiger." He stepped inside. "How are you doing?"

"Very well, thank you. I see you still have wonderful manners."

Matt smothered a grin. What was it about an old lady that made him feel like a ten-year-old all over again?

"I come bearing cake." His lifted the box aloft in one hand as proof.

"Just bring it on through to the kitchen. That's where Rachel is," she replied with a wave of her knobby hand. She raised her voice a quavery octave and hollered, "Rachel, that cake has arrived!"

Matt paused and inwardly winced. After his refusal of the party invitation, he wasn't looking forward to Rachel's reaction to seeing him standing in her kitchen. He didn't have much of a choice, though, so nodded his thanks and headed on through.

Rachel didn't see him at first. She stood with her back to the doorway, three drawers pulled open, and she was rooting through one of them. Matt cleared his throat.

"Thanks, just—" Rachel turned, and when her eyes landed on him, she stopped short.

"Doug asked me to drop it by. He got caught up with another order," Matt said by explanation. "Sorry to crash the party."

"Crash it?" She smiled. "I'm glad you're here. Would you—"

"I'm not staying," he interrupted, sliding the cake onto one side of the table. The other side was occupied by a large metal tub, filled to the brim with ice and cans of pop.

"Just do me one favor?" She looked at him pleadingly, her dark eyes pinned on him. "Then I'll let you go. I promise."

"What do you need?"

Rachel jutted her chin toward the metal tub. "I need

to get that thing out to the backyard. I can't lift it, and if I let the uncles at it, they'll get hernias."

Matt chuckled. "Sure. For the uncles' hernias."

Rachel flashed him a grateful smile. "My cousin very helpfully put it all together for me on the kitchen table and then took off for a date."

"Thoughtful," he said with a grin.

"Very. Two of my uncles already offered to carry it, and I was told in no uncertain terms that if those old men end up broken, I'll pay for it."

"You have a lot of family in the area," he said, glancing out the kitchen window. Some older men—the uncles, he assumed—stood around a dartboard, and on the other side of the yard, a few younger couples chatted. Kids wove their way around everyone else in joyful abandon.

"No better way to catch up with everyone," she said, turning back to the drawers.

"What are you looking for?" he asked.

"A black plastic slotted spoon—" She snatched it up in a victorious swoop and banged the drawers shut. "Aha. Shall we?"

Matt hoisted the heavy tub, grimacing with the weight of it, and Rachel opened the back door ahead of him, holding it open as he stepped through. The tub was ridiculously heavy, but his male pride wanted to hide that fact from Rachel. There was something about her sweet smile and grateful eyes that made him want to show off like a high school kid. He put the tub down next to a table of food, repressing the grunt as he stood up again.

"I'm so glad you came when you did," Rachel said, putting a cool hand on his arm, her touch lingering only for a moment before she pulled away again. "Thank you."

"My pleasure."

She looked up into his face, hesitant. "Do you have other plans tonight?"

He'd been pretty determined to steer clear of this birthday party, if that counted as plans.

"I forgot those notes here when I fixed the drain for you," he replied. "I need to brush up a bit before I do a kids' summer camp presentation tomorrow at the library."

"Chris is going to that day camp tomorrow," she said. "Did you want me to come see you do the presentation so I can give you some tips?"

If only it were just another presentation.

"Actually this is the one where I'm being observed by a member of the hiring committee, so…" He shrugged. "But I appreciate the offer."

"Oh…" She was silent for a moment. "You'll do well. You're good, Matt—better than you give yourself credit for."

"You've helped more than you know," he said, grappling for the words to express what was inside him, but he couldn't quite grasp them. "Thank you," he concluded gruffly.

"Let me get you those papers," Rachel said. "They're on top of the fridge."

Rachel led the way back into the house and then headed back into the kitchen. As the screen door banged shut behind them, Chris came around a corner, a fistful of cookies in one hand.

"Hi, sweetheart. Having fun?" Rachel asked.

He nodded. "Yeah. Do you know Uncle Walter? He knows lots of stuff!"

Rachel blanched and put her hands on her son's cheeks, tilting his face upward. "Sweetie, don't listen too closely to what Uncle Walter says, okay? We'll talk about him later on, after everyone's gone."

"Okay," the boy replied uncertainly, and then he shot Matt a grin. "Hi, Mr. Bailey. It's my birthday again."

Before Matt had a chance to answer, the boy was off again. Rachel shot Matt a rueful smile. "Uncle Walter has dementia, and he's been known to say some pretty inappropriate things. I'm hoping he wasn't telling Chris about his air force days, because otherwise…" She made a face.

Matt chuckled. "He'll probably survive it."

"I'm more worried about him repeating it in Sunday school," she said with a laugh and pulled down a bag of balloons and the papers from the top of the fridge. She handed him the papers with a grateful smile. "I'm sorry. I noticed them earlier and put them up there for safekeeping."

"Thanks." He took the papers and rolled them into a tube. "You're a good mom, Rachel."

Color tinted her cheeks. "I forgot the balloons."

Matt nodded out the kitchen window. Chris stood next to one of the uncles, a smile sparkling in his eyes. The boy leaned over to look at a pocketknife the old man held out for his inspection, and he said something they couldn't hear—something that made the old man laugh in good humor. "See that?"

Rachel's gaze followed his, and she paused.

"He's happy," Matt said. "You're doing a good job. He

doesn't need a hundred balloons, or streamers, or whatever else. He needs this—family. His mom."

Rachel's eyes misted and she met Matt's gaze. "Thank you."

"Go on," he said. "Go enjoy this with your son. A pile of balloons isn't going to make a bit of difference to that kid. Trust me."

Rachel nodded and pulled her hair away from her face. "I think I will. Thanks. And I hope tomorrow goes well."

"Thanks." Their eyes met for a moment, and he found himself thinking about stepping closer, but he knew better than that. "Take care."

Matt paused for a moment, watching her as she headed out the back door. Her dark hair swung around her shoulders, and the melodious tinkle of her laugh filtered back into the kitchen as she bent down and gave Chris a squeeze.

She was a beautiful woman, that much Matt had to admit, and as he watched her standing with her family, he pushed away the image that popped into his mind—a picture of himself standing there with her, an arm around her waist as they asked the uncles if they wanted another soda from that massive metal tub of ice that was likely now melted down into a solid brick in the warm afternoon.

"You the boyfriend?"

Matt glanced down at an old man who peered up at him questioningly.

"No. Just a friend."

"Oh, sorry." The old man shrugged. "You never know. She might look your way if you stick around long enough. I'm Walter."

"Uncle Walter." Matt shot him a grin. "Nice to meet you."

"You play checkers?" the old man asked.

"I actually have to get going—" Matt began.

"Come on. One game." Walter waggled his bushy white eyebrows comically. "I'll even let you win. Say, are you a military man?"

I'm not getting out of here, am I? Matt thought ruefully and followed Uncle Walter back into the living room. One game with an old-timer. Then he was leaving.

Rachel looked around the house at the paper cups, the wadded napkins and the scattered pieces of birthday wrapping paper and heaved a happy sigh. The party had been a great success. Everyone had fun, most of all Chris, who lay on the couch, snoring softly. He clutched a book, a birthday present from an aunt, under one arm, and she bent over him, smoothing his hair away from his forehead.

"Do you want help cleaning up?" Matt asked.

Rachel shook her head. "I'll do it tomorrow." She shot him a tired smile. "Thanks for staying. I feel bad. You were supposed to be at home brushing up on your presentation."

"I couldn't have left if I tried," he said with a laugh. "Your uncle Walter wouldn't let me out of his sight."

"Oh, Walter…" Heat rose in her cheeks. "I hope he didn't say anything too inappropriate."

"Well, I now have a working knowledge of a bomber jet," he replied with a soft laugh. "And I've been schooled in checkers."

"That's a relief. It could have gone worse."

Matt opened the front door and Rachel followed

him, taking a quick peek back at her sleeping son on the couch. As they stepped out onto the porch, a warm breeze circled around them, lifting Rachel's hair away from her face.

"Walter sure is a character," Matt said, humor flickering in his eyes.

"Oh, you have to tell me what he said," she groaned. "I'll imagine something much worse. Put me out of my misery."

He laughed. "It wasn't that bad. He seemed pretty focused on teaching me how to formally court a woman."

"Formal courting?" She raised her eyebrows. "Huh. I didn't see that coming."

"What does he normally talk about?"

"Don't ask." She felt the blush in her cheeks. Uncle Walter normally told stories from the war—the sorts of "adventures" that men hid from their wives once they got back on American soil again. In Uncle Walter's case, that was all before he met his wife, but in his declining years, Uncle Walter's memories were back in his bachelor days.

"I feel bad that I didn't bring Chris a gift," Matt said.

"Oh, don't worry about that." She shrugged and leaned her back against the porch post. "He was swimming in presents."

"I guess so." He looked down at his feet, his brow furrowed, then raised his eyes to meet hers. "I've got something, though."

"Oh?"

Matt reached into his shirt pocket and pulled out what looked like a Polaroid picture. He looked at it for a long moment, then passed it over.

"What is it?" she asked, but as she looked closer, she

knew exactly what it was. It was a photo of Matt holding Christopher on the night that he was found. Matt looked mildly panicked with the baby in his arms, but there was also a certain amount of satisfaction in those dark eyes, as well. His muscled arm supported the slight weight of the newborn, and Chris snuggled against his rescuer's broad chest, sound asleep in the same position he used to sleep on her chest when she brought him home.

"Oh, Matt..." she whispered, tears rising in her eyes. "I didn't know you had this."

"One of the guys gave it to me today," he admitted. "I thought Chris might want it."

"*I* want it." The words came out before she could stop them, and she gave him a bashful shrug. "Is that bad to admit? I do, though. This is the first happy memory we have for Chris, and now we have a photo of it."

"It was a special night," he admitted, his tone low and deep. "I never thought I'd see him again."

"Funny how life works, isn't it?"

For a long moment they were silent. He stood close enough to her that the warmth from his chest emanated against her arms. Down the street, a dog barked, and farther away another answered. The soft light from the window spilled over their feet, but their faces remained in shadow. It felt more comfortable that way, somehow, as the velvety night closed in around them.

"I meant to stay away tonight," he said softly.

"Why?"

"Because of this. Here. The moonlight, the summer wind." He reached forward and brushed a strand of hair away from her eyes. "You."

"Am I such a danger?" she asked.

"Yes."

Rachel laughed softly and looked out at the yard—the long shadows made by the moon and the green eyes of a raccoon peering at her from the bushes. "I thought I was being nice."

"You are. Too nice. I'm doing my best to leave town, you know."

"I know." She brought her eyes back to his face and gave him a sad smile. "And I'm not stopping you."

"I'm at the head of the running for that position. As long as I can do well with a presentation to schoolkids tomorrow, I'm pretty sure I've got the job."

"Congratulations." She forced a smile and nodded quickly. "You deserve it."

"I'm not as excited as I thought I'd be."

"No?" She tried to force some cheerfulness but failed. "I'm sorry. You're my first friend here in town, and I'm going to miss you."

"Me, too." He sighed. "If things were different—"

"You don't have to say it," she said quietly. "It's okay. They aren't different."

He nodded, and they fell into silence again, listening to the quiet sounds of the summer night. Rachel couldn't help the melancholy thoughts that rose inside her. She thought of her husband, who died too soon, of her son, whose birth mother hadn't been able to care for him, of her attempts to rebuild a life for her little boy, and now of Matt, who had wormed his way into her life and who would be off to new adventures just as soon as he could manage. She felt lonely standing there, because no matter how solid and reassuring he felt right now, this wouldn't last. Why was it that the sweetest things in life felt the most fragile?

"Hey." Matt's voice rumbled deep, and he put a finger

under her chin, lifting her gaze to meet his. She realized in that moment that a tear had escaped and trickled down her cheek. She sniffed and dropped her gaze, smiling to cover that tear, but he moved closer. He didn't speak again, and when her gaze flickered up to meet his, his warm lips came down onto hers in a kiss as light as a moth's wings.

Rachel didn't move, not forward, and certainly not away. He smiled and when she parted her lips and sucked in a wavering breath to say something—something un-planned and meaningless, she was sure—his lips came down onto hers once more and her eyes fluttered shut.

Matt's warm, calloused hands slid down her arms, and for a moment everything but the two of them melted into the velvety darkness of the summer night. His hand came up to her face, and as he pulled away he touched his forehead to hers.

"Sorry," he whispered gruffly.

"It's okay."

A smile came to her lips and she met his gaze with a soft laugh. Before she could say anything else, a rustling sound at the door made her heart skip a beat.

"Mommy?"

Chris stood in the doorway, a perplexed look on his face. He looked from Matt, back to Rachel and asked haltingly, "What are you doing?"

"Nothing, Chris," she said quickly, casting Matt a look of alarm and hurrying to the door. "Let me get you up to bed, sweetheart. It's late."

Rachel looked back once more to see Matt, his eyes clouded with unnameable emotions, standing on the ve-randa. He stood balanced on the stair, about to step out into the night. He didn't leave just yet, and his steely gaze seemed to hold more words and thoughts than he'd ever expressed to her. She felt momentarily torn between her maternal instincts and the man with the strong shoulders and brooding gaze who stood on her porch. Matt raised his hand in a silent wave and then headed down the stairs and out into the night. Rachel stood with her son in a living room littered with the vestiges of a birthday party, her heart filled with the memory of Matt's gentle lips pressed against hers in the cool evening air.

"Let's get you upstairs," she said softly, taking Chris by the hand. "My poor tired boy…"

As she climbed the stairs behind her son, she prayed earnestly, *Oh, Lord, let Chris forget this by morning!*

The next morning, Rachel yawned, tucking the phone between her shoulder and cheek. She held a garbage bag in one hand as she ambled around the first floor of her home, picking up wrapping paper, napkins, plastic cups and various litter from the evening's celebration. She looked skeptically down at a pair of reading glasses that had fallen into the couch cushions. They would belong to one of the aunts, no doubt. She'd have to call around later on that morning, seeking the half-blind owner.

"He kissed you!" Louise exclaimed on the other end of the phone. "When did this happen?"

"After all of you went home," Rachel replied. "It wasn't planned."

"The best kisses aren't." Louise chuckled.

"It was a stupid thing to do. I know it. He has other plans, and I certainly can't be getting into another relationship. At least not right now."

"I know, I know." Louise sounded impatient with old excuses. "You're worried about Chris. But part of parenting is protecting children from too much information. He doesn't need to know anything is even happening between the two of you. It isn't that complicated. Just be discreet."

"He saw us," Rachel admitted.

"Oh." Louise sighed. "Well, you're in a lurch, aren't you?"

"That's all you've got?" Rachel asked with a wry laugh. "No wisdom?"

"I'm afraid not. You'll have to tell me how you handle it all."

Rachel chuckled and dropped the half-filled garbage bag onto the ground at the door to the kitchen. "I haven't decided what to do yet, but I'll fill you in when I do."

"Your son is your top priority," Louise said quietly. "And that's a good thing, but you do realize that one day he'll be all grown up and you'll be left on your own, right?"

"Not for some time," Rachel replied with a short laugh.

"Faster than you'd think, dear. Time flies, and when these little boys grow up to be men, they act like men and they no longer need or want their mommies in their business. You want to be a good mother, and I agree with you that you must, but you also have to take care of yourself. You have to have a life of your own in place when he's a grown man and ready to fly the nest."

"I don't even want to think about him being an adult yet, Auntie."

"I know." She laughed softly. "But trust me—you deserve a romance of your own, too. If not Matthew Bailey, then someone else."

Rachel was silent, her mind working over her aunt's

advice. She knew that Chris would grow up, and her deepest fear was that once he was a grown man and no longer needed her, he'd resent her for not being enough, not doing enough when he needed her most. She hadn't considered that he might resent her for smothering him with her love.

"Well, your uncle just woke up. I'd better get him some coffee," Louise said. "Just think about it, dear. Talk to you later?"

After Rachel said goodbye and hung up the phone, she picked up the garbage bag once more and moved into the kitchen, continuing her quest for random trash.

Father, she prayed, *what do I do now? I know I'll have to have my own life when he's a grown man, but he's just little now, and he needs me more than he even realizes. I feel like a failure already.*

It wasn't entirely fair, and she knew it, but maternal guilt was a wily beast. From a successful birthday party where her son finally relaxed and seemed to settle in with his aunts and uncles, to catching his mother kissing "his firefighter" on the porch… She grimaced and covered her eyes with one hand. There was no point in waiting around the kitchen. She grabbed the last of the paper cups from the counter and swiped them into the bag, then tied it shut and dropped it by the door. Then she headed up the stairs toward her son's bedroom.

Easing open the door, she found Chris lying on his bed, eyes open and hands behind his head. He looked over at his mother, his usual exuberance dampened.

"Morning, sweetheart," she said.

"Hi, Mom."

She'd been hoping that he might have been too sleepy

to remember last night's kiss, but that hope was shattered by the tone of his voice.

"Do you want to talk about yesterday?" she asked softly.

"Why were you kissing Mr. Bailey?" Chris asked, propping himself up on one elbow.

Rachel sat down on the side of his bed and took a deep breath. She'd always thought she'd be more cautious than this, and she'd introduce someone special to Chris before he ever suspected that she was involved. This situation was completely out of control.

"Sometimes when a man and a woman care about each other, they show it with a kiss," she said.

"Like when they have babies?" Chris asked.

"No!" Rachel shook her head vehemently. "That's something different. That's for a husband and a wife. Mr. Bailey and I are only friends."

"But you don't kiss Pastor Gord, and he's your friend, right?"

Rachel smoothed a hand over Chris's hair. "No, honey, you're right. It's different. Mr. Bailey and I have gotten to be very good friends, better friends than I am with Pastor Gord."

"So, is Mr. Bailey going to marry you and be my new dad?" Chris asked.

"No."

"Why not? I thought kissing was when you love somebody."

"Well…" Rachel sighed. "Sweetie, there are some grown-up reasons why Mr. Bailey and I can't go any further. Last night, we probably shouldn't have kissed each other, but we did. I'm sorry that you saw it."

"So you don't love Mr. Bailey?" Chris asked.

His question was so innocent, and her answer should have been quicker, but she found herself wondering what exactly she did feel for Matthew Bailey. It was certainly more than friendship, and she'd relived that kiss a hundred times between last night and this morning. She was holding herself back from feeling more than she should, and she wasn't sure that she was really succeeding all that well.

"Mommy?"

"I…care about Mr. Bailey a lot. I hope that he can be our friend for a very long time. And I'll keep from kissing him again, okay?"

"Does Mr. Bailey love you?"

"I haven't asked him."

"I don't want you to have a boyfriend," he said somberly. "I don't like Mr. Bailey anymore."

"Well, then, you're in luck." She bent and kissed his warm forehead gently. "I don't have a boyfriend, and you still have your firefighter. Nothing has changed."

Chris didn't answer. He stared out the window morosely, his cherub lips puckered in a pout.

"Now get up. I'm going to make you some bacon and eggs, and then you start your day camp at the library."

Chris eyed her dubiously.

"It'll be fun," she said, ruffling his hair. "You'll see. More fun than staring at me all day. If you stay home with me, I'm going to put you to work." She shot him a playful smile, but he didn't respond.

Rachel stood up and went back to the door. "Come on," she coaxed. "I'm starting the bacon now, and if you aren't downstairs in time, I'm eating it without you."

That succeeded to get the boy moving, and he kicked back his covers and bounded out of bed. Another day had just begun.

Chapter Nine

A large group of schoolkids poured into the library's activity room. They came in, laughing and swatting, giggling and pushing—a swarm of overly excited, sugar-hyped children who were far enough into their summer holidays to be officially bored with anything less than a circus. One window spilled some natural sunlight into the room, and fluorescent lights hummed overhead, illuminating a mottled carpet and eggshell-white walls decorated with a few posters about the adventures of reading. Matt couldn't say that he was looking forward to this.

"All right, kids, settle down," one of the college-aged day camp leaders called. "Let's get quiet, guys."

The children took their time finding a place on the floor to sit down, and Matt looked from Firefighter Johnson, who stood next to a pile of his fire gear, to Mr. Bernard, who sat in one corner, a tablet in hand and an eerily calm expression on his face. Sweat glistened on his forehead and dampened his dress shirt under the arms—the room was far from comfortably air-conditioned.

Abe Bernard's judgment of today's activities would

make or break Matt's chance at this job, and that knowledge put an edge on an already stressful day.

Rachel's advice came to mind, and he scanned the group of kids, sending up a silent prayer for help. Not guidance. Not wisdom. Not insight. He wanted Help. Capital *H*. Toward the door, away from the eyes of the group leaders, Matt saw Chris, seated cross-legged and glowering in his direction. He had a pretty good idea about what was upsetting the boy, and he sighed, putting his attention back into the job at hand.

"Good morning!" Matt said, raising his voice over the hubbub. "My name is Deputy Chief Matthew Bailey, and I'm here to tell you about fire safety. But I want to start with a question. How many of you have ever seen a fire?"

The presentation went about the way he had expected it to. About three-quarters of the children paid attention at one time, but when he started suiting up Firefighter Johnson, starting with his boots and pants and working their way up to his air tank, helmet and visor, more seemed to find the presentation interesting. Professionally, this was a relief for Matt because this was the part of the presentation that was life-and-death, whether the kids realized it or not. By showing the children the amiable firefighter and then putting him in his gear, he was showing them that a big guy in a fireproof yellow suit carrying an ax wasn't someone to be afraid of—he was someone to rescue them.

At the back of the room, Chris scowled steadily in Matt's direction, but Matt couldn't help noticing when a bigger boy nearby Chris leaned toward him and whispered something. He wouldn't have taken notice if it weren't for the way the color drained from Chris's face, and Matt's pulse sped up. He knew that look.

"Now I've got a question for you," Matt said. "How many of you kids know what to do when a fire alarm goes off?"

Hands went up, and a buzz of conversation started.

"You, in the back." Matt pointed at the boy next to Chris. "What's your name?"

"Aaron."

"Hi, Aaron. So, what would you do if there was a fire alarm right now?"

"I don't know," the boy replied.

"How about you?"

Matt kept the group moving, but he didn't miss it when the boy leaned toward Chris again and whispered something that made Chris's jaw clench and his eyes snap. Without missing a beat, Chris turned and punched the bigger boy square in the face.

The fight was on, and the boys scrambled and threw blind punches. The two women who were acting as day-camp counselors moved in. The room was in an uproar. One of the young women looked entirely daunted, and the other was focusing on Chris.

"Christopher, I saw you hit him," she remonstrated, and Matt bit back his anger. Chris wasn't to blame with this one, but apparently they couldn't see that. He had a choice: step in and take care of this himself, or let them blame Chris. Matt glanced at Firefighter Johnson.

"Take over, would you?" he said.

Stepping over the other children, Matt put a solid hand on both boys and hauled them apart.

"Both of you, outside that door," he barked.

The boys wiped at their noses with the backs of their

hands and obediently slumped from the room. Abe Bernard looked ready to follow.

"Thanks, Abe, but I'd rather take care of this one alone," he said with a tight smile.

The older man nodded and made a note on his pad, and Matt stepped outside, pulling the door shut behind him. Jeff Johnson's voice took up the rest of the presentation, and Matt walked the boys through the library and out into the sunshine.

"What happened in there?" he demanded.

The boys were silent.

"I'm serious. Sit down." He motioned to a bench, and both boys sat down as far from each other as possible. "Now, I'm not blind. What did you say to him, Aaron?"

"Nothing" came the reply.

"Chris? What did he say?"

"He said my real mom didn't want me," Chris muttered.

Matt froze. Could the gossip have flown that quickly?

"Where did you hear that, Aaron?" he demanded.

"Everyone knows it. He's the kid whose mom dumped him off at the fire station. His mom gave him away."

Matt heaved a sigh. "Aaron, it's wrong to make fun of someone for being adopted. Being adopted doesn't mean he isn't wanted. In fact, his mother wanted him so badly that she chose him."

"His mom *now*," Aaron retorted.

"And she's his mom." Matt's tone grew icy. "Now for you, Chris. Hitting is never the answer."

Chris hung his head and didn't say a word.

"I know you got mad, and Aaron said some pretty bad stuff, but you never have to hit someone. Do you understand me?"

Chris nodded, his guilty gaze flickering up to Matt's face. "Yeah. Sorry."

Chris wasn't the one Matt was worried about, though, so he turned to the other boy.

"Aaron, I'm going to discuss this with your mom and dad, and I don't want to hear that you're picking on other kids again."

"It's what my dad said," Aaron muttered.

He'd definitely be speaking with Aaron's parents, now. Matt put a cap on the rising anger inside him.

"Your dad and I can discuss that. Now make up with Chris right now and you both say you're sorry."

The boys grudgingly faced each other and mumbled apologies.

"Like you mean it," Matt said, his tone sterner.

"I'm sorry I said that," Aaron said.

"I'm sorry I hit you," Chris added.

"Good." Matt heaved a sigh. "Now you can both go back in."

The boys scuffled back toward the main library door and Matt stood outside in the hot noon sunlight. He wasn't ready to face the classroom full of kids just yet, and he glared out into the parking lot. Was this the way Chris had been treated in his last school? How on earth had the news of Chris's birth spread that quickly through Haggerston? The last thing he wanted was to have Chris picked on for the rest of his schooling, and he could certainly understand why Chris had thrown the first punch.

The library door opened, and Matt glanced up to see Chris coming back outside. He slowly walked up to where Matt stood, staring down at his shoes.

"What's the matter, Chris?" Matt asked. "Are you okay?"

"Yeah."

"Are you sure?"

Chris dug a toe into the pavement. "I don't want to go back in."

"Why not? Still mad?"

"I guess."

"If you give Aaron a chance, he might end up being your friend."

"What if he keeps bugging me?"

"He won't. I'll have a word with his parents." He leaned over, giving Chris a grin. "His mom is pretty tough. You should see her."

"I mean, what if he keeps bugging me in school?"

"Then you—" Matt stopped himself from saying, *Then you come to me,* and licked his lips. "Then you tell your mom right away, and she'll know what to do."

"I don't know…"

"Your mom is really smart, you know. You should give her a chance. Schools don't let kids bully other kids."

So why hadn't the other school stepped in sooner and fixed this before it got out of hand?

Chris looked up at Matt skeptically. "I saw you kiss my mom."

Matt rubbed a hand over his eyes. "Yeah, I noticed that."

"She's not your girlfriend, you know," Chris announced. "She doesn't want to be."

That statement stung, and Matt pressed his lips together, choosing his words carefully. "It wasn't your mom's fault, Chris."

"How come you did it?" the boy demanded.

"Because she's pretty and smart. And she's got a really nice laugh, and she's kind. You know what a wonderful person your mom is, don't you?"

"Yeah," Chris admitted reluctantly.

"Well, I think she's pretty great, too. So I kissed her."

"Are you sorry?" Chris asked skeptically.

Matt chuckled and looked out over the library parking lot. "No, Chris. I'm not sorry I did it. I'm sorry that it upset you, though."

Chris only looked partially mollified and they stood with their backs to the library, facing the parking lot with a scattering of cars and pickup trucks. A soft breeze whispered around the building, but it wasn't enough to compensate for the heat of the high sun.

"Look, it isn't my business, Chris, but one day your mom will probably want to get married again."

"She doesn't need to," Chris said. "She's got me."

"And you're a great kid. But don't you want a dad one day?"

"No."

Matt chuckled softly. "It's okay, buddy. Your mom loves you a whole lot and I have a feeling she wouldn't take that step unless you were ready for it."

"Do *you* want to marry my mom?" Chris asked, eyeing Matt cautiously.

Matt pressed his lips together. "You don't have to worry about that, buddy."

It was an evasive answer, and he knew it, but announcing to the kid that the idea of coming home to Rachel every day was pretty pleasant wasn't going to smooth anything over today.

"Are you going back in to be with the other kids?" Matt asked, glancing down at his small companion.

"Nope," Chris replied.

Matt pulled out his cell phone. "I guess I'd better call your mom, then, so she can pick you up."

Rachel pulled up in front of the library and heaved a sigh. She'd driven five miles an hour over the speed limit to get here as soon as possible, but now as she parked the car, she wished she had a few more minutes to think this through. The sun shone unforgivingly down on the little brick library, shining onto the heads of the big firefighter and the small boy who stood out front.

More fighting. That was the thought that hung prominently in her thoughts. Her son, her sweet boy with the bright eyes and captivating smile, was fighting out his frustration again. How could she fix this?

Matt stood next to the boy, his arms crossed over his chest like a soldier on duty. His gaze was steely, but when Chris said something, his expression softened and he leaned closer. They exchanged a few words and Matt nodded and gave a weak shrug. Even though she couldn't hear their words, she was fiercely grateful for that small gesture of gentleness toward her boy, and she pushed open the door and slammed it with a bang.

"Hi," Matt said as she reached them.

"Hi." She sighed. "So…how is everything?"

Matt looked down at Chris, who remained studiously silent, an expression of exaggerated innocence on his face. She knew that look well.

"You said he was fighting?" she asked.

"Yeah."

Matt looked down at Chris again, seeming to give him a chance to say something, but she knew her son better than that. Chris stared up at her mutely.

"Thanks," she said. "I'll take care of it." She was

used to these calls by now, and while she had no idea how she'd take care of it, she knew that whatever was chipping away at her son was her responsibility. She reached out and put a hand behind his shoulder, nudging him toward the car.

"Wait." Something flickered in Matt's gaze and he glanced down at Chris. "You mind if I explain it to her, buddy?"

"I guess not," Chris muttered.

"It wasn't all Chris's fault. The other kid was a bully."

"What happened?" Rachel dropped her hand and Chris edged back again.

"The other kid was making fun of the fact that Chris is adopted."

She winced. "Why are children so cruel?"

Matt glanced down at Chris. "I talked to the other boy, and I'll have a word with his parents about it. I doubt he'll be bugging Chris again."

Rachel sighed, relieved that someone seemed to be taking Chris's side for a change. He'd gotten a reputation for being "the bad kid" in his last school, and it had gotten to the point where any scuffle that happened was deemed Chris's fault. She bent down in front of her son.

"So he teased you about being adopted?" she asked quietly.

"He said my real mom didn't want me."

Real mom. Those words stabbed, and she attempted to hide her reaction with a smile. "I am your real mom, sweetie."

"I know. But my other mom."

She nodded. She knew exactly what he meant—she just wanted to nab the title of "real mom" for herself. "So you hit him?" she asked softly.

Chris nodded.

"Remember how we talked about this before? You've got to tell a grown up, remember? A grown up can help you to sort it out. If you hit someone, no one cares what bad thing they said. They only care that you hit. Hitting doesn't solve anything."

"Sure it did," he retorted.

"And what did it solve?" she asked, shaking her head.

"He stopped, didn't he?" Chris said with a victorious smile. She smiled wanly in return.

"We'll talk more about this later." She stood up and pulled a hand through her dark waves. "Chris, I left a snack for you in the car."

"What is it?" he asked skeptically.

"A bologna sandwich," she said. "Your favorite. Why don't you get your snack at the car while I talk to Mr. Bailey a little bit, okay?"

Chris looked ready to argue but shrugged his thin shoulders instead. "Okay."

He headed over to the car and Rachel touched the unlock button on her key fob with a responding beep from the car. She watched him silently, her heart full of anxiety, sadness and an overflowing abundance of love for her troubled boy.

"You okay?" Matt asked.

"I'm fine," she replied with a sigh. "I'm worried about Chris. He's—" She swallowed. "I was hoping a change in scenery might make a difference for him."

"I have a feeling he was upset about more than the comment," Matt said slowly.

"You mean, last night," she concluded.

"Yeah. He talked to me about it, man-to-man."

"Oh?" Rachel eyed him in interest. "What did he say?"

"He basically told me to back off," Matt replied with a low laugh. "And I'm not to consider myself your boyfriend."

Heat rose in Rachel's cheeks and she shook her head. "He has enough to deal with right now."

"I know." Matt put his hands into his pockets and looked out into the parking lot beyond Rachel, his blue eyes clouded in thought. "He's a sensitive kid, and I know you don't want to hear this, but I was kind of relieved to see him belt the kid."

"Why would you say that?" she asked. "This was the problem in the other school. He kept fighting. He fought everyone, and no one could figure out why. I thought someone might have been picking on him, but the teacher insisted that Chris was the one to start it. I've been working so hard with him, trying to show him that hitting isn't the answer."

"Look, there are two kinds of boys." Matt dropped his gaze down to meet hers. "There are the boys who get picked on and curl up into a ball, and there are the boys who get picked on and stand up for themselves. I'm not saying that punching another kid is the answer, but at least he's standing up for himself. He's not beaten."

Rachel nodded. "Are you trying to make me feel better?"

"Nope." He shot her a wry grin. "Just calling it like I see it."

Rachel smiled, rolling his words over in her mind. "So you don't think I have as much to worry about as I think I do?"

"I think he'll be okay."

She sighed. "The thing is, in the other school, *he* was considered the bully."

"But why was he lashing out?" Matt asked.

"That's the million-dollar question, and he wouldn't say. The teacher had already decided he was trouble, and I think that had something to do with his reluctance to talk. By the end of the school year, I was just glad to have him out of that school and safe at home with me for the summer." She glanced up as the library doors opened and a portly man carrying a suit jacket over one arm came toward them at a leisurely pace. Matt glanced in the direction she was looking, and she noticed the tension rise in his posture.

"Hi there," the man called.

"Abe Bernard, this is Rachel Carter," Matt said, looking between them. "Rachel is Chris's mom."

"Ah, the fight." Mr. Bernard nodded sagely. "Is it all taken care of now?"

"Looks like," Matt replied. He turned toward Rachel. "I should probably get going."

Rachel nodded quickly. This was obviously the man from the hiring committee, and a feeling of regret rose inside her. If Matt didn't get this job, she didn't want it to be because of them.

"Abe, how about I meet you in the truck? I'll just be a minute."

Abe nodded, gave a polite salute to Rachel, then headed away from them.

"The interviewer?" Rachel whispered.

"That's the one."

"And you came out here and talked things through with Chris and me instead of showing what you could do in there." She jutted her chin in the direction of the library.

"Yeah, well…" Matt shrugged.

"Matt, this might not be good for your chances. You shouldn't be putting us before your interview. You want this."

Matt was silent for a moment; then he shrugged. "I saw the look on Chris's face, Rachel. He needed a hand."

Tears misted her eyes and she blinked them back. "Thank you, Matt. You're a really good guy."

A smile crinkled around his eyes and he brushed a hand over her shoulder. "I'd better get going."

She nodded, and Matt caught her eye one last time. "Don't be too hard on the kid."

"I won't."

As Matt sauntered off toward his truck, Rachel turned in the other direction, heading back toward her car, where her son waited, his cheek full of sandwich.

"Let's go home, sweetheart," she said quietly.

"Are you mad at me?" Chris asked cautiously.

She glanced at her son, the last crust of his white-bread sandwich in one hand and his big blue eyes fixed on her face.

"Not mad," she said, reaching into the backseat to give his knee a squeeze. She started the car, then craned around to see out the back window as she reversed out of the parking space.

Lord, help me, she prayed in her heart. *It's starting again, and I still don't know how to fix it.*

That evening, Matt stood in his kitchen, a cup of hot coffee between his palms. It had been a long day. Mr. Bernard had chatted with him briefly after the library presentation, then driven off in the direction of South Maitland in a swirl of dust, and Matt had a sinking feeling that his hopes of getting out of this town had left with him.

He took a slow sip of coffee, inhaling the comforting aroma. Was it so bad to miss out on this chance?

An image of Rachel rose in his mind—her hair damp from the rain, springing up into curls around her face. Her eyes were bright, her cheeks pink, and he thought— not for the first time—of the feeling of her warms lips against his.

Lord, could I really just walk away from her...head out of town and never look back? Or would I regret that for the rest of my life?

He was thirty-five and still single, so he knew exactly how rare and beautiful it was to find a woman who made him feel the way Rachel did. Maybe there was a silver lining to being passed over for the South Maitland fire chief position. He wasn't on his way out of Dodge, but at least he'd be close by Rachel and Chris for a little while longer. Maybe he could help Chris get a handle on the bullying situation before he left, too.

Matt found himself feeling almost cheerful about the whole thing, and he picked up the most recent pile of mail that he'd left on his counter and sorted through the envelopes. There were a few bills, a couple of envelopes addressed to Occupant, which went directly into the trash, and the local newspaper. He shook the paper open and glanced over the front page.

Three Years after Fatal Fire, Broxton Park Elementary to Reopen.

The headline was followed by a full-color photo of the school in flames next to a new snapshot of the school now, ready to open once more to the surrounding community. He closed his eyes, the old tension closing in around his heart.

"Just stop!" he barked aloud, slapping the paper against the counter, then tossing it into the trash. How long was this town going to rehash this tragedy? Was it horrible? Absolutely. He saw it almost every night in his dreams. Was it senseless? Of course. But the journalists writing these articles didn't seem to care what their constant rehashing did to anyone else. They were simply scraping around, looking for a topic that made the town of Haggerston look even remotely newsworthy. Haggerston was a sleepy little place with nothing to report but the canned preserves contest at the local fair and the Quilting for Equality program that a few church ladies had started up to raise money to give to charity. Haggerston wasn't even remotely newsworthy until the fire, and now the reporters stuck in this town wouldn't let up.

They hadn't tried to save her. They hadn't been the last one to look into her terrified face before she went limp. What right did they have to haul up her memory every other month in order to make a headline in a small-town rag?

Except no one else was complaining, so who was he to get indignant with a town that wanted to hold on to little Natalie as long as possible?

He put down his coffee with a thud and sucked in a deep breath.

I don't think I got this job, Father, and I don't know how I'm going to stay here.

God knew what he needed. He knew what this was doing to him. Why was it so hard to leave his future in God's hands?

His cell phone rang, and Matt glanced down at the number, ready to press Ignore, but he froze when he saw the number. It was South Maitland. He let out a pent-up breath and picked up the call.

"This is Matt Bailey."

"Hi, Matt." Mr. Bernard's voice was cheerful. "I'm probably calling during your dinner hour, aren't I?"

"No, no, it's fine," Matt said with a wry smile. "I haven't even started cooking yet, so you're safe."

"Oh, that's a relief. My wife told me I should hold off and let you eat in peace, but I said, 'Margie, his food will go down like sawdust anyway, so I might as well call.'"

Matt chuckled good-naturedly. "She meant well."

"She always does. She always does." There was a pause. "Well, I wanted to let you know that I met with the board when I got back, and we took the vote."

"Oh?" Matt tried to keep the hope from seeping out of his tone, but he wasn't successful. He closed his eyes and winced. Being all hopeful would only make it worse when he had to pretend it didn't matter too much.

"As you know, you ranked very highly in our estimation," Mr. Bernard went on with agonizing slowness. "You have the education, the references, the experience and pretty much everything we were looking for on our list for the perfect fire chief. When I came to observe you in action, I expected to see a little more action, however…"

Here it comes.

"I was surprised when you left the rest of the presentation with the captain under you. On my drive back to South Maitland, I had some time to think, though, and I realized that two young boys matter just as much as a whole group, and a fire chief's position is about fire safety, but it's also a position of respect and leadership in a community. You took the time to help two little boys sort out their conflict. You cared, and you put them in front of your own professional aspirations. I respect that."

"Thank you, sir."

"I told the board about what happened, and they agreed that it showed character and compassion, and we voted unanimously to offer you the position of fire chief of South Maitland."

"Wait—" Matt swallowed hard. "You're offering me the job?"

"Yes, we are. Congratulations, Mr. Bailey. Now it's your turn. What do you say?"

Matt looked down into the trash can at the newspaper, the image of the flaming school uppermost on the pile of garbage, where orange flames and pouring black smoke fought for dominance over the page. He scrubbed a hand through his short hair.

"Thank you, Mr. Bernard. I'm honored, and I'm happy to accept."

"Excellent!" Mr. Bernard crowed. "I'll let the board know that we have a new fire chief for the town of South Maitland. I'll come down to Haggerston with the papers to sign tomorrow, if that works for you."

"Perfect," Matt said with a nod. The sooner the better. "I'll see you then."

Hanging up the phone, he sucked in a breath, searching his gut for a reaction to this. He felt nothing—nothing at all.

Lord, he prayed in his heart, *You've given me the job, the way out. Thank You.*

Yet somehow he knew he couldn't just walk away

from Rachel, either. God might have given him the professional step up, but what about Rachel? What about the baby he'd pulled from a soggy cardboard box seven years ago and bonded with against his better judgment? Where did they fit into his future?

He picked up the phone and dialed the number of his direct boss, the Haggerston fire chief. Even if he left town, he had an idea of how he could provide a little more stability for the two of them.

Chapter Ten

As Rachel and Chris approached the fire station the next afternoon, she stopped Chris and put a hand under his chin.

"What?" he asked.

"You have jam on your face." She licked a finger and wiped the smudge of raspberry jam from his cheek while he squirmed away. She chuckled and looked down into his face. "You're growing up. You're not my tiny boy anymore, are you?"

He shook his head. "Nope."

"But I'm still your mom." She ruffled his honey-blond hair. "That's not going to change."

He gave her a lopsided grin. "Will we get french fries?"

"What does that have to do with a visit to the fire station?" she asked with a laugh. "No. We'll go home for soup and grilled-cheese sandwiches later."

Chris pondered that for a moment, then turned toward the front door of the station. "Okay."

She was relieved that everything seemed so ordinary today, from the leafy trees spreading overhead to the rambling form of her son, heading toward the now familiar door of the fire station. When Matt had called the night before and asked her to meet him at the station to talk about a possible contract position with the fire department, she was intrigued. She'd been making her peace with her husband's death over the past few weeks, and working with a fire station no longer rankled as it would have before. Besides, as a single mother, she had only her own income to rely on, so beefing up her take-home pay could only benefit her and Chris.

"Hi," Matt called as they came into the front door. "Come on through."

He beckoned them in, and Rachel shot the receptionist a smile on her way by. Chris dawdled behind, and she turned, putting a hand on her hip and giving him The Look. His pace quickened, but as soon as she looked away, he slowed again.

Rachel sighed and pulled her hand through her hair. Dragging a seven-year-old anywhere was an event. She ended up feeling exhausted and beaten.

"Tough day?" Matt asked, keeping his voice low.

She nodded. "Yeah. It's all part of being a parent, I'm afraid."

"Hey, Chris," Matt called. "Let me take you and your mom up to the gym where the guys work out to get their big muscles. What do you say?" He lowered his voice again. "Then maybe you and I could talk."

Chris perked up that thought and picked up his pace once more, and Rachel glanced up at the big man next to her, wondering what he had in mind. He had refused to elaborate on the phone.

"How much can you lift?" Chris asked, looking up at Matt with new respect in his eyes.

"More than you." Matt chuckled.

"Could you lift my mom?"

Matt's gaze softened as he glanced down at her, and Rachel felt the heat rise in her cheeks in spite of herself.

"You bet," he said with a shrug. "Right up over my shoulder. Want a demonstration?"

"Yes!" Chris laughed.

"No!" Rachel chuckled at the same time, taking a precautionary step back. "No demonstrations on me, thank you very much."

Matt held her eye teasingly, then laughed, the sound echoing through the halls. He led the way up the stairs toward the crew room, Chris at his heels.

"This is the training room," Matt said.

Some easy chairs were lined up around a large-screen TV, one of which was occupied by a big fire-fighter who was watching a training video that showed a car in flames. A table was in the center of the room, piles of training material lining one side of it. A CPR dummy stared cheerfully from a corner where it was propped up. Two firefighters sat at the other side of the table, open binders in front of them, and when Matt entered the room, every man present snapped his attention toward their boss.

"Just passing through," Matt said with a nod. He led the way farther down the hallway and pushed open another door. "This is the gym."

Chris stepped inside and watched in mute admiration as another firefighter lifted weights. He was a big man, with a thick neck that melted into even more massive shoulders. He looked as if he could bench-press a house if absolutely necessary.

"Can I watch?" Chris asked.

"Sure." The big man shrugged. "I don't mind."

Chris stood back as the firefighter lifted the heavy barbell, grunting with effort with each flex. Rachel shook her head with a smile. This was the sort of thing a mom couldn't provide. No kid ever bragged that his mom could lift a piano, and she'd always been okay with that, but the older Chris grew, the more she realized that he was a boy, not a baby, and he was going to have to learn to navigate the world of men.

"Nathan's a good guy," Matt reassured her, and they stepped outside the room.

"It's guy stuff," she explained. "He loves muscles and trucks and…" She cast around for another word. "His latest interest is wrestling."

Matt chuckled. "Not your thing?"

"I'm his mom." She shrugged. "Try as I might, I can't be his father, too. And trust me, I try."

"So, how are you holding up?" Matt opened the door next to the workout room, and they stepped inside. It was a quiet space with shelves of books and a writing desk. A small window let in a shaft of sunlight that pooled at her feet.

"I'm doing all right," she said. "Haggerston is starting to feel like home already."

"I'm glad." Matt leaned back against the desk and regarded her thoughtfully. "I suppose I should just come out with it."

She stayed silent and looked up at him cautiously.

"I've been offered the job in South Maitland."

His words brought a mist of tears to her eyes, and she blinked them back hurriedly. This had been the plan all along, and she didn't blame Matt for wanting out of town. She understood his motivation perfectly, but somehow the disappointment stung more than she'd expected.

"I can't say that I'm surprised," she admitted quietly. "They'll be fortunate to have you."

"Yeah…" He cleared his throat. "I talked to the fire chief here in Haggerston last night, and he said that they could use a seasoned teacher on a part-time basis to help out firefighters with presentations. It could make the team that much stronger. I suggested you."

"That's really kind…" She swallowed hard. "I'll have to think about it. Is it being offered to me?"

"If you're interested."

Rachel moved to a table and leaned against it, her mind sorting through the information. It was a good offer—one that would make a financial difference in her home—but her heart was still stuck on the first thing he'd said: he got the job. Matt followed her lead and leaned next to her, his muscular arms gently brushing her sleeve. She looked up at him, tears misting her gaze again.

"I'm sorry, Matt," she said, swallowing hard. "I really am happy for you. I'm just…" She searched for a word.

"Me, too." His words were gruff and he nodded quickly.

His gaze was still fixed broodingly on the opposite wall.

"This wasn't supposed to happen. I wasn't supposed to get attached." She sucked in a breath.

"Yeah, I thought I had that under control, too." He reached over and took her hand in his warm palm. "I guess I'm not as tough as I thought."

How had this happened? How had she managed to fall in love with another firefighter? She knew better than this! She wasn't a naive twenty-year-old this time. She was a grown woman with a son of her own. Yet Matt wasn't like Ed at all. It seemed to be only the job that they had in common.

"You're very different from my late husband," she admitted.

"Yeah?" He squeezed her hand. "How so?"

"You're..." She blushed. "You're not the type of man I'm used to." How could she tell him that his conventional good looks were a little intimidating for her? She was used to a man who had unconventional looks, an inner strength that was based in his character. She was used to wearing flats and blending in with him. But when she was with Matt, she didn't feel as though she blended in with anything... Not in Matt's eyes, and not in anyone else's, either.

"It's not that I'm a wallflower, exactly," she confessed. "But being out with you is different than I've been used to. People notice you."

"It's not me they're looking at," he said with a slow smile. "They're all pretty used to seeing me around."

Rachel shook her head. "See? Like that. I'm sure you're used to making women swoon with stuff like that. I'm used to being with a man who has no idea how to make a woman swoon and he does it by accident."

"You think I'm some sort of ladies' man?" He sounded mildly offended. "Just ask anyone who knows me how much I date."

"No." She sighed. "I'm intimidated."

"By me?" His voice softened.

"Not you exactly," she tried to clarify. "By us. By how I feel when I'm with you."

"I wish I could tell you to get used to it," he said softly. "Because you'd be safe with me, babe."

The endearment made her breath catch in her throat, and for a moment, she thought of what it would be like if he bent down and kissed her, but she cleared her throat and dropped her gaze.

"But you're leaving." She nodded, repeating the words more to convince herself of them than to communicate anything to him. She pulled her hand out of his warm grip, her fingers feeling suddenly cold outside his grasp.

"Yeah," he said quietly. "But you could come along."

"What?" She shot him a shocked look. "What do you mean?"

"Come with me." He turned toward her, his clear gaze locked on hers. "I make enough to keep the three of us. Just come along."

"I don't just move with men. I mean, we aren't married."

"I know." He heaved a sigh. "I just want to find a way to keep you with me."

She let her gaze wander around the room, stopping at the sunny window. She stared at the bright scene outdoors for a moment, none of the details impacting her memory. Then she turned back. "You can't stay, can you?"

He shook his head slowly. "That fire, Rachel, it was…" He sighed. "I need a fresh start. I'd love to make that fresh start with you."

She understood. Yesterday's paper had more pictures of that fire emblazoned across the front, and when she'd seen it, her first thought had been for Matt. It would stab him, and she knew it, and she understood exactly why he wanted to escape.

"I know I've been blaming this on Chris all along," she admitted, her voice low. "That isn't fair. It's just an easy excuse, I suppose. It's true that Chris couldn't handle all this right now, but it's more than that. I can't be a firefighter's wife again, Matt. I just can't."

"Even a fire chief's wife?"

"It's the same—" Tears welled up in her eyes. "The job will always come first."

"What do you mean?"

"It's public service!" Her voice trembled with emotion as she met his eyes. "I've been down this path before. The job always comes first. When that siren goes off, your priority is the fire, and I get that. It has to be that way. I just hate it!"

"Someone has to do the job."

"I know that, but I know better this time around. The first time, with Ed, I thought it would be romantic. Well, I've done it once, and I don't want to come in second again." She shook her head. "Even now you can't stay. I know exactly why you can't stay—that fire, little Natalie, the memories—but it doesn't change the fact that a job is coming first."

He didn't answer at first; then he slowly shook his head. "You think I'm putting you second? Is that it?" He stood up straight and came around to the front of her, his clear blue eyes blazing straight down into hers.

"Yes!" she retorted. "You are. You might not have a choice. What firefighter ever has a choice? But yes, I'm coming in second, and I'm tired of that life. I'm tired of being the one left at home to worry while the man in my life heads off to save someone else's family!"

He closed the gap between them and his lips came

down onto hers, smothering her words. He pulled her closer, and she let herself melt into his strong arms. His lips pressed tenderly over hers, and as he pulled back, his hand moved up to her cheek. She leaned her face into his palm, wishing desperately that her answer could be different. Her voice broke, and she cleared her throat.

"Isn't it worth a try?" he asked.

"A relationship is hard work. It's not all rose petals. If I feel this frustrated with the job right now, it isn't going to change. I know that."

"What if stayed?"

"Stayed?" She frowned. "Would you?"

He hesitated. "I could…for a little while."

"A job like the one in South Maitland doesn't come along every day." She shook her head. "I can't let you sacrifice that. You'd only resent us. Your life isn't here, and I know it."

"And yours is," he concluded.

"It has to be. This is for my son."

"And I can't change your mind on that?"

"I'm so sorry, Matt. But no." The room felt so small and smothering, and she sucked in a breath, trying to ground herself once more. She was a mother. She had responsibilities. "Maybe we should find Chris."

Silence stretched between them for a beat, and Matt nodded.

"Yeah, let's go find him." His tone was low and wooden. She looked up into his face once more, reading the pain and regret in his features, mirroring her own. As she passed him and moved toward the door, his broad hand warmed the small of her back while he guided her past him. She wished she could stop and lean into those strong arms of his again, but she propelled herself forward.

So this is what it feels like to break up.

Matt let Rachel leave the room ahead of him, his heart heavy. He wanted to pull her back, to wrap her in his arms again and see if just holding her close could fix anything. He knew better. He couldn't stay, and she couldn't be the wife of a firefighter. Why was it that the first time he felt like this about a woman, it was impossible for them to be together? This wasn't how he'd imagined this last night. He'd hoped that she'd agree to come with him and that they'd be happily planning their future right now... He sucked in a breath, pushing back the surge of sadness as he followed her into the hallway.

Rachel looked into the gym next door and shot Matt a perplexed look.

"He's not there," she said, worry edging her tone.

Matt frowned and looked inside. Nathan was working on his back muscles, doing a dumbbell incline row—an exercise Matt was more than familiar with. With a grunt, the other man looked up inquiringly.

"Where did the boy go?" Matt asked.

"Went to get you, he said," the man replied.

Matt glanced back at Rachel in the hallway, and they exchanged a worried look. Was it possible that Chris had been listening to their conversation in there? He inwardly grimaced. If the kid hated the idea of him kissing Rachel, then how upset would he be when Matt asked her to move with him?

"Did a little boy come through here?" he heard Rachel ask down the hall. There was a muffled reply, and Rachel came back toward him, her eyes clouded with worry. She shook her head in answer to his unspoken question.

"The only other way out was down the back stairs," Matt said. "This way."

He led the way to a narrow staircase and they jogged down the stairs to the hallway below.

"Chris?" Rachel called, raising her voice loud enough to carry. "Where are you?"

There was no reply, and he could sense Rachel's anxiety rising. She took a deep breath and headed off in the direction of the garage.

"Chris?"

Matt angled over to the reception area, and the receptionist looked up with a professional smile that faltered when she saw his face.

"Everything okay, DC?" she asked.

No, everything was not okay. Everything had managed to implode in the last fifteen minutes.

"Did a little boy come through here?" he asked brusquely.

She shook her head. "No. Is he missing?"

"I'm sure we'll find him." His reassurance was meant for Rachel, not the receptionist. He'd been the one distracting her…asking for more. "If he comes this way, call me, okay?"

The receptionist nodded and rose from her desk, looking out the door that led outside. She shook her head to indicate that she didn't see anyone outside.

"I'll keep an eye out, sir."

Matt met Rachel back in the hallway. She turned in a full circle, her dark eyes filled with worry.

"He's around somewhere," Matt reassured her. "He

couldn't have gone far, and he hasn't been past reception. I wouldn't worry too much."

She nodded but didn't look any less concerned. Before he could say anything else, the piercing fire alarm whooped through the building. He put a hand out and pushed Rachel back against the wall, just as two firefighters, clad in boots and fire-retardant overalls, sprinted down the hall.

"But Chris—" she started.

"Stay back." He didn't mean to bark at her, but the trucks would pull out in another forty-five seconds, and slowing the firefighters down simply wasn't an option. The trucks' sirens started up and wailed mournfully as they pulled out of the garage. Rachel looked up at Matt.

"Okay," he said. "Let's take one more look around."

Ten minutes later, Rachel's eyes filled with anxious tears.

"Where could he have gone?" she demanded. "You don't think he saw us—"

"I kissed you. It isn't against the law," Matt said, shaking his head irritably.

He wasn't even hiding his feelings anymore, and if Chris had seen them, he'd feel personally responsible if the boy took off because of it. He knew that Chris was fragile right now. He wanted to protect the kid, not freak him out.

"Well, he's not here." Her voice quavered. "I know he didn't go out through reception, but he's not in this building."

Matt had to agree. "All right. Let's drive around the block and see if we can spot him."

Matt led the way to his pickup, and they both hopped in. Matt took a moment to scan the street around them.

A couple of cars cruised past, and a paperboy on a bike meandered down the side of the street, a bag slung across his body and a rolled newspaper in hand.

"Hey!" Matt called. The boy turned, cautiously curious.

"Did you see a little boy around here? About this tall—" he measured with his hand on the side of the truck "—wearing blue shorts and a red shirt. Blond hair."

"No, sir."

"Thanks." Matt slammed the door shut. Obviously he wasn't good with kids if he didn't see this one coming. He'd been in there kissing the boy's mother, asking her to uproot her life—and Chris's—in order to move with him across the state. It all seemed ridiculously obvious now. What boy wouldn't take off under those circumstances?

"I'm sorry, Rachel," he said, his voice low as he pulled out onto the street.

"It's not your fault," she said with a sigh. "He knows better than to take off. Trust me, when I find him, there are going to be some consequences."

Matt smiled wanly, but a sick feeling settled in his stomach. The kid was seven years old. It didn't matter if he knew better or not. Sometimes the consequences to a kid's dumb choice were worse than any parent could inflict in punishment.

Father, let us find him, he prayed fervently. There was no way anything was going to happen to Chris on his watch.

"Does he know the way home from here?" Matt asked.

She shook her head. "I don't know. We could try."

"Does he have a favorite place to go when he's upset?"

"Not yet. We haven't been here long enough."

He pulled out his cell phone and dialed with a thumb. Punching the speakerphone button, he dropped the phone into his lap.

"Chief Taylor here." Greg Taylor was chief of police and a personal friend.

"Greg, I've got a situation here," Matt said. "A boy is missing. Seven years old, wearing blue shorts and a red T-shirt. He was last at the fire station and seems to have evaporated. Can you issue an Amber Alert?"

"You bet," Greg replied, his tone turning terse and professional. "What's the boy's name?"

After a quick back-and-forth to give all the information, Matt hung up and looked over at Rachel. Her peaches-and-cream complexion had turned sallow and wan, and her lips were pressed together into a thin, frightened line.

"All the patrol cars will be watching for him, too," Matt said. "He's not going to get far."

Rachel nodded, scanning the road as they drove along.

"I've got an idea," Matt said, pulling over to the side of the road and making a U-turn.

"Where are you going?" she asked.

"To the fire."

"The one the trucks left for?" she asked, darting him a sharp look.

"He didn't leave through the front door, doesn't know any back exits and isn't in the firehouse. We've circled this block twice. It's remotely possible that he was in a truck."

"*In* a truck?"

He shrugged. "If I were seven, that's the first place I'd explore. The fire trucks."

She nodded and sagged against the seat. "Maybe. It's worth a try."

Matt could only pray that he was right, and as the tires spun in the gravel at the side of the road, he cranked the steering wheel and gunned the motor.

Lord, please, let us find this kid before— He couldn't finish that thought. God knew what he meant and knew where Chris was. That would have to be enough. His training was taking over now, and the sick flopping feeling in the pit of his stomach was covered by a professional calm.

"He must be terrified," Rachel said, turning stricken eyes onto him.

"We'll find him." His tone was curt, and he gave her a tight smile. "Hold on."

He cranked the steering wheel again and spun around a corner. He knew the location of the fire well—an old house at the west end of town. The back way was faster—not for a full fire truck, perhaps, but definitely for a versatile pickup. He slapped the siren on as he came toward a four-way stop and sailed through without even touching the brake.

The smell of smoke tinged the air as they came closer, and when Matt pulled up onto a side road, he could already hear the pulsing thud of water from the massive hoses attached to the truck. Rachel was out of the truck before he even came to a complete stop. Slamming the truck into Park, he kicked open his door and was a few steps behind her as she ran up to the crew captain.

"Excuse me—"

"Ma'am, I need you to get back, please."

The house was an old-fashioned, three-story mansion-style home from at least eighty years ago. The sad thing about these old places was that without proper updating, they were death traps, and this home had been deemed uninhabitable at least a decade ago. A new buyer had been in the process of renovating the place until recently, it seemed. A large town-provided garbage bin sat in the middle of the drive, old wood and scaffolding poking out like mangled limbs. Smoke poured out of broken windows, and from the inside, Matt could make out the sound of firefighters breaking down doors. They had to be sure they'd covered every room inside, just in case someone might be in there.

"Ron!" Matt barked, and the crew captain turned flinty eyes in Matt's direction.

"Sir? Something wrong?"

"Have you seen a boy around here? He's about this tall—" he measured in the air "—red shirt. Blue shorts. Blond hair."

"A kid?" another firefighter called from his position at the truck with the hose connection. "I saw a boy who looked like that. He was upset. He saw a cat in the window."

"Where is he now?" Rachel demanded.

The firefighter shook his head. "I told him to get back, and he did. I don't know where he is now."

"I think I do," Rachel breathed, and her gaze turned miserably toward the flaming house.

"Do you think he would?" Matt asked, his voice low.

In reply, she turned red-rimmed eyes onto him, her pale lips quivering.

Without another word, Matt broke into a run. His gear was in the back of his truck, where a deputy chief always kept it. In a matter of minutes, he was suited up.

"Ron, I'm going in. I think the kid might be inside."

Matt adjusted the visor over his face. Fifty pounds' worth of gear weighed his body down so that every move he made was intentional and he wasted no energy. The inside of his thick fire-retardant jacket was already heating up, his own body heat acting like a convection oven, and sweat sprang up along his spine and down his chest.

"I've got Turner doing a left-hand search," Ron said. "You take the right, sir."

"Will do."

Matt jogged to the front door and looked back at Rachel, who stood motionless and pale, staring after him. A mother on the sidelines.

He shook off the pressing memories and stepped inside, mentally leaning back on his training to carry him through. Emotion was a great thing in life, but it hampered a man with a mission. This wasn't about Natalie. This was about Chris, and this was a different day.

The pounding thud of spraying water and firefighters' voices reverberated through the house. Inky darkness swallowed him up, and he reached up to turn on the light on his helmet. It snapped on, shooting a welcome beam of light ahead of him. Matt edged along the right-hand wall, his shoulder brushing gyp rock as he moved.

"Fire department!" he called as he came to the first doorway. "Chris? You in here? Anyone?"

Silence reflected back at him, and Matt moved into a room that appeared to be the living room, empty of furniture except for some painting scaffolds that he had to maneuver around. A pile of paint cans and drop cloths dominated one corner, and he felt through them, searching for the soft flesh of an arm or leg through the mounds of fabric. He scanned the floor, searching for any sign of Chris—a shoe, a hand…anything. As he exited the room, he picked up his pace. If Chris was in this house, there wasn't much time. Smoke killed faster than flames.

"Fire department!"

He moved into the next room—the kitchen. Cupboards rose like coffins and he flipped the first few open. They weren't big enough to hold a child, but he wasn't taking chances.

"Chris?" he called. "Are you in here? It's Matt. I'm going to help you."

Silence. He keep his breathing as calm as possible. He only had thirty minutes of air on his back, and if he got excited, he had even less time before going out to grab a new air supply. Dark smoke swirled around him, and he swatted the cupboard doors open, then pulled open the fridge. It was empty.

Moving around the room, he came to the back stairs and headed on up. Turner was on his way down.

"Turner!" Matt called. "Anyone up there?"

"Empty, sir," came the reply.

"I'm double-checking just in case."

"Okay."

Matt moved past the other big man on the narrow staircase, his heavy boots echoing through the house as he mounted the stairs. As he emerged on the second floor, he followed the right-hand wall again, moving into one bedroom after another. They were all empty, closets hanging open and dripping with water, scorch marks streaking up the walls. The last bedroom reverberated with the thud of water, and as he came inside, Gordon looked up and raised a hand in salute.

"That you, sir?" he asked.

"That's me," Matt replied. "Looking for a kid."

"No sign, sir."

He didn't know if that was good news or bad news. A fire was a dangerous place to be, but a lost or abducted child was horrible, too. Matt headed out once more, but as he came into the smoky hallway, movement flashed in the corner of his eye. He stopped, images flashing through his mind of that blue shoe he'd seen in the Broxton Park school hallway... He pushed it back, willing his mind back to a state of calm.

Not here. Not now, he warned himself.

He looked around. He was in some sort of sitting room, also empty of furniture, but next to a window, an orange calico cat crouched in terror. He could only imagine that it was the cat that Chris had seen. He moved slowly toward the animal.

"Hey there, puss," he said softly. "Come on. I'll get you out."

The cat looked ready to bolt, but at the last second, he snatched her up by the scruff of her neck. She hung frozen in the air until he pulled her close against his chest, half under his arm to keep her secured. There were no more rooms to check, and he pushed the button on his radio.

"Ron, I'm done with the right-hand search. I'm coming out. Over."

"Affirmative. Over."

Matt paused, listening.

Lord, if he's in here, show me where.

Nothing else moved, but the cat struggled in his grasp.

With a sigh, he angled his steps toward the staircase and headed back down, feeling with the heel of his boot for the back of the stair so as not to fall down the staircase in the murky darkness. Overhead, he heard the other firefighter radio in his completed mission.

"Sir, the fire is out. I'm on my way down. Three minutes of air left. Over."

He reached the bottom of the stairs and turned toward the front door, then stopped, looking back. The kitchen stood empty, the cupboard doors all open the way he'd left them. He felt as if he should see something—a hat, a hunched little back. He couldn't leave this house if he thought there was any chance he was leaving Chris inside.

Nothing. The room was empty.

He's not here. Lord, where is he?

Turning back toward the front door, Matt clomped over to the fire hose and broke into the afternoon sunlight. Sweat beaded on his face and trickled down his neck. Salt tasted on his lips, and he pushed back his visor, eager for a natural breeze.

Rachel stood in front of him, her wide eyes fixed on his face.

His own grim expression mirrored hers.

He wasn't there.

Chapter Eleven

Rachel heaved a shaky sigh. She knew she should be relieved that her child wasn't in a burning building, but all she felt was devastated when she saw Matt emerge from the smoky building, his arms empty, save for the cat.

"He's not in there," Matt sat, pulling his mask off with his free hand, his gaze meeting hers. His hair hung wet with sweat around his face. The cat squirmed in his grasp, and he stroked its head gently with one gloved finger. "But he *was* here, Rachel. We're closer than before."

She nodded, and she glanced toward the truck. Her heart ached inside her chest with a wave of despair. Rachel shut her eyes, searching for God's calming presence, and as her eyes fluttered back open again, a small, grubby hand slid into hers.

"Mommy?"

"Chris!" Rachel dropped to her knees and pulled her son into her arms, squeezing him tight and burying her face into his neck. She held him for a long moment, then pulled back, sniffing back her tears and examining him from his dirt-streaked face down to his dusty knees and scuffed running shoes. "Where were you? How could you just run off like that?"

"I was looking at the trucks and then the alarm went off and…" Chris looked toward Matt searchingly. "I didn't mean to."

"But you left the workout room and didn't tell me," Rachel said, shaking her head. "That was really wrong. I was worried sick. What if something happened to you?"

"Yeah." Chris looked down. "I just wanted to see what was down the stairs."

And when he'd gotten there, he'd found a seven-year-old boy's pot of gold—the fire trucks. She could see it all unfolding in her mind's eye.

"Do you even know where you are right now?"

"No."

"Well, it's a good thing that Mr. Bailey thought to look for you here. I didn't know where to look. If it weren't for him…" She swallowed the awful images that rose in her mind. She'd have searched around the firehouse. She'd have gone back home to see if he were there. She would have called the police. She might not have found him for hours—hours of torturous worry for a mother. "Don't you do that to me again." Tears welled up in her eyes and she pulled him back into a hug. "Do you hear me? Never again."

Chris nodded against her cheek and when she released him, he looked up at Matt.

"You got the cat!" The boy's face broke into a grin. He wriggled free of his mother's arms and reached up for the animal. Matt put the cat down and it streaked under a truck and he slowly undid the clasps of his heavy fire jacket.

Chris went after the cat and stopped at the truck. He

crouched down next to a big wheel as he peered after the frightened feline.

Rachel wiped her eyes with the back of her hand and shook her head. "That's ten years off my life right there."

"I believe it." Matt's voice was warm and deep. "You okay?"

She nodded. "Now."

Matt tossed his jacket over a stump. His sweat-streaked face, the heavy suspenders holding up his fire-retardant pants, the big boots on his feet—they all came together into one reassuring whole. She looked gratefully up at this big, gentle man who had just torn into a burning building to find her son, and she smiled tentatively.

"You really are Chris's firefighter," she said.

"Not just his..." Matt held out his hand and she stepped into his muscled arms. He squeezed her close, so close that it almost hurt, and she felt the roughness of his stubble catching against her hair.

"Well, he's safe and sound," Matt said quietly.

"Yeah." She leaned into the musky warmth of his chest. "Thank you, Matt."

A simple thank-you didn't encompass all she felt in that moment. The depth of her gratitude couldn't be captured in words. He'd done more for her in the past hour than she could have expected from any other man, and she looked up at him questioningly.

"You went above and beyond, you know that, right?" she asked.

Matt dropped his arms and gave her a boyish smile. "What could I do?"

She smiled through the mist of grateful tears. "I don't know how I could possibly thank you for today."

"No need," he said with a shake of his head. "I'm just glad he's safe. That's enough for me."

"Would you do me one more favor?" she asked.

"Of course."

"Take us home?"

Matt nodded. "Let's go." He looked at his watch. "I'm signing the papers for that job in less than an hour."

Her own smile wilted on her lips and she nodded quickly. Of course he was. This was the plan all along, wasn't it?

"Chris!" Rachel called, trying to keep the waver from her voice, and the boy stood up from his crouch by the fire truck's massive tire. "Come on, sweetheart. We're going home."

Chris ran along beside them as if he'd just had an ordinary afternoon. He was a resilient kid—more resilient than she was in this situation. She slid an arm around his shoulders and pulled him against her side.

"We're going home and we're staying put for the evening, okay?"

Chris nodded.

Matt opened the door to the truck and her son hopped up into the cab. Rachel followed and pulled the door shut with a bang. Behind them, the fire trucks roared to life and the men were winding up the last of the hose. Matt heaved his fire gear into the back of the truck, then ambled around to the driver's side. As he settled into the driver's seat, he shot Rachel a smile over Christopher's head.

"You kept so calm," Rachel said as he pulled out to the road.

"Training. It comes in handy."

She smiled as they eased out onto the gravel road.

"It's harder parenting alone. There is only one set of eyes watching. I miss being able to rely on my husband to watch for him, too."

Matt nodded but remained silent. His eyes flickered in her direction, then fixed back onto the road.

Stupid, she chastised herself. He'd offered to be more—did he think she was toying with him now?

"I didn't expect you to react like that," Rachel said instead.

Like a dad, she thought. Or as close to a dad as Chris had experienced in the past four and a half years. She'd been so cautious to keep men out of Chris's life who might get his hopes up for something more that she'd forgotten what a relief it was to have a partner in these things—a man to balance out her perspective and to be a shoulder to lean on when she was worn-out.

"Neither did I." His voice was so low that she almost didn't catch his words, and she looked over at him, surprised.

"I thought the training took over," she said.

A smile flickered at the corner of his lips. "A little more than training."

She'd suspected as much, and the admission brought a smile to her lips and caution in her heart simultaneously. She pressed a kiss against the top of her son's head and sighed. Was it terrible to wish she could go back to the simpler days before school and fights, and that simmering frustration inside her little boy?

The gravel road turned into a main street, and before long Matt signaled onto the street that led to Rachel's house. The familiar street brought a comforting warmth to Rachel's heart, and her eyes trailed over the houses of her neighbors. She glanced up at Matt. So this was it.

Rachel patted Chris's leg.

"We're home," she said softly. "Thank Mr. Bailey."

Matt eased into their driveway and the truck crunched over the gravel, then stopped.

"Thanks, Mr. Bailey," Chris said.

He had no idea how much he owed to his big, protective fireman. One day, she'd have to make sure he understood.

"Thank you, Matt," she said as she climbed out of the truck. There was so much more to say, but she didn't know how to put it into words right now.

"Don't mention it." His tone was low and he looked at her for a long moment. "Take care."

He would go sign the papers. He would move to South Maitland. His life would go on, and so would hers. This was for the best, but why did it have to hurt so badly?

Matt didn't speak again, but he raised two fingers in a salute. Rachel raised her hand and blinked back tears. She held those tears back as his truck backed out of her drive and disappeared down the street.

Chapter Twelve

Matt slammed the heels of his hands into the steering wheel and pressed his lips together into a tight line. So this was it—he was going to sign the papers that guaranteed him a fresh start. His dream job, far enough away from this town for him to try to forget.

I could stay.

But could he? Perhaps for another year or so, but not indefinitely. He wasn't a naive young man, and he knew better than to expect that a beautiful woman could fix his problems.

They warned against that in the therapy the fire department provided. He'd gone to exactly one session. He was there long enough for the therapist to nod thoughtfully and say, "Mr. Bailey, you can't do this forever. You'll crack. And when you do, you'll take it out on your wife and children. So you'd best deal with this now. It's better than ruining what you love most, isn't it?"

But at that time in his life, he had neither wife nor child, and he highly doubted that a few chats about his feelings were going to change anything. Natalie was dead. It was a fact, not a feeling. So he'd thanked the therapist for her time and left, and never did go back. He could deal with this alone, he'd thought. He could fix the torn parts inside him if he just had enough time and a little bit of privacy.

Well, South Maitland was his attempt to fix it. A fresh start. A new town. A new community to protect and settle into. Haggerston would never forget Natalie Martin, nor should it. Natalie deserved to be remembered, but he couldn't stay for the constant reminders of his own failure.

God, I really wanted something with Rachel, he prayed silently. *I could have walked away from Haggerston and never looked back, except now she's here, with Chris.*

Maybe it was better to move on before he got more attached. It had only been a few weeks. People didn't feel this strongly after such a short period of time, did they?

He shoved that ache further down into his gut and signaled a left turn. The tires spun on the gravel as he made the corner just a bit too fast, dust billowing up behind as he sped up again.

Peace Hills Christian Church rose out of the prairie grass like a relic. This would be his last visit to the Peace Hills Cemetery, and he thought that before he signed those papers he owed Natalie something—a goodbye, at least. An apology for not being able to handle a longer vigil in that town.

He eased into the small parking lot in front of the church and parked. He sat in silence in the vehicle for a few moments, then heaved a sigh and got out.

A hot summer wind rolled across the plains and blasted him along with the bare gray church. He headed around the side of the building toward that familiar little grave by the corner, ensconced in the scent of heavy, nodding bunches of lilacs.

Her grave marker was half in the shade and half in the sun, a wilted bouquet of flowers sitting on the sunny side. He squatted down onto his haunches, his gaze moving over the etched marble.

"Is that you, Matt Bailey?"

The voice startled him and his head snapped in the direction the voice had come from.

"Mrs. Martin."

The middle-aged woman stood by the church, her hands covered in floral-patterned gardening gloves. Her chin-length graying hair was pulled back in a ponytail, wisps of which fell free around her face. She pushed some hair away from her forehead with her wrist.

"Wendy," she said. "We've known each other too long for formalities, Matt."

Matt nodded, giving her a tight smile. "Wendy. I'm sorry. I probably shouldn't have come here."

"Why not?" She stepped closer and looked up at him, her eyes, lined from life and the sun, moving over his face probingly. "You've come before."

"I didn't realize you'd seen me."

"You looked like you needed some privacy," she said. "I come here to keep up the graveyard quite often. I feel the same way I did when I'd clean Natalie's room."

Matt smiled and shrugged. "I didn't mean to intrude."

"You aren't intruding. Why do you keep saying that?" She nodded in the direction of a bench in the shade of the church building. "Do you want to come sit?"

Matt looked from the grave to the bench, casting around for some excuse to get out of the little visit, but considering that he'd be leaving town, he thought perhaps he owed something to Wendy Martin, too. He nodded and followed her toward the bench.

"I know you and I have a bit of history," Wendy said quietly. "I've done my best to show you how sorry I am for that."

"I'm not upset with you, Wendy. Don't worry about that."

"I don't blame you. I was just so—"

"You don't need to explain again. I know. It's okay." He looked across the freshly mown grass toward the rows of graves. A large cross rose in the center, the grave of a wealthy parishioner, it seemed, already forgotten by everyone but direct family.

"The fact is, I let you down," he said quietly. "I've wondered repeatedly how many seconds I wasted, how much faster I should have been to have gotten her out in time."

Wendy was silent for a stretch, and she shook her head. "I'm grateful for what you did."

"I failed her."

She frowned slightly. "Here is what I know. My daughter was in the middle of a fire, alone, frightened and in pain. She could have died there all by herself, but instead she saw a fireman coming to her rescue. She was confused and afraid and tried to run away, but he scooped her up anyway, and her last conscious memory was of being rescued. My daughter did not die alone, Matt, and that is because of you. For that I will always be grateful."

Matt nodded slowly. He'd done his best, but it just hadn't been enough. If Natalie's mother could forgive him, could he forgive himself? He wasn't sure.

"There's going to be a park opened in Natalie's name," Wendy said. "Will you be there for the opening?"

Matt clenched his teeth and shook his head. "No."

"I thought you might want to—"

"No." His tone grew stronger. "Wendy, I know you're grieving, but I have to stop. I hope you find comfort, but it doesn't do much for me, all these vigils and memorials."

Wendy blinked; then slow recognition rose in her eyes. "You've done all those public appearances for me, haven't you?"

"Of course," he replied gruffly.

"It wasn't for you, then."

"Me?" He shot her a quizzical look. "How could it have been for me? I stood in front of this town as a reminder that I didn't do the job I'm here to do. I was the one who wasn't fast enough."

"Oh, Matthew…" Wendy's eyes filled with tears and she put a maternal hand over his. "I'm sorry."

"You have nothing to apologize for, ma'am."

"But I do," she said softly. "Everyone understands what I lost. I lost my little girl, and that was the worst hell I could possibly imagine. Everyone understood that."

He frowned, uncertain about what she was getting at.

"You, though," she continued softly. "You lost Natalie that day, too. She might not have been your daughter, but you still lost her. And you've had to grieve, too."

He didn't answer. Instead he watched a bumblebee lumbering above the head of a yellow daisy. It buzzed quietly, hovering heavily before landing on tiny feet on the ruffled center.

"*Have* you been able to grieve for her, Matt?" Wendy asked hesitantly.

"It's hard to grieve in the public eye," he replied quietly. "You can probably understand that."

"Come." Wendy held out motherly arms.

Matt's eyes widened in alarm. "Pardon me?"

"Come here," she commanded. "This is like at funerals, where we hug each other and cry together. You had a huge loss, too. And I'm sorry for everything that *you* lost."

Matt bent cautiously and Wendy wrapped her arms around his neck, gently patting his back the way she might soothe a small child.

"It'll get better, Matthew," she said softly into his ear. "I promise. It'll hurt less and it'll get better."

Matt nodded, tears rising in his throat. He swallowed them back and braced himself, fighting against the deep sadness that threatened to sweep over him. Wendy released him and rose from their seat on the bench.

"I'm going to go home now," she said quietly. "You take all the time you need with Natalie."

Wendy bent to pick up her bucket of gardening tools, then walked resolutely away, leaving Matt alone in the small graveyard. He stared toward the tiny grave in the far corner, and all the sadness he'd shoved down over the past three years pushed defiantly upward past that cap he'd placed deep inside himself. Haggerston needed him to be their steely hero, and he'd obliged, but the therapist had been right. He couldn't be their hero forever— something had to give.

Tears broke through his guard and he dropped his head into his hands, unable to control the sobs that shook his broad shoulders. He cried for Natalie, a girl who should have been able to grow up. He cried for her parents, who had to face the death of their own child, and he cried for his own loss, too. He'd lost more than a little girl who'd looked to him for rescue; he'd also lost his naive confidence in his own abilities. Sometimes, even when he did everything right, he wasn't going to be enough.

When his tears were finally spent, he found himself lighter than he'd felt in the past three years. He didn't feel alone as he sat on that bench. He could feel God hovering close, closer than he'd ever felt in his lifetime. He looked for a few moments at the little grave, now completely covered in shade, and he wiped his face with his palms, sucking in a deep breath of lilac-scented air.

"Goodbye, Natalie," he said quietly as he pushed himself to his feet. "Rest in peace."

This was the closure he needed. He wouldn't come back.

Chapter Thirteen

Rachel pulled the last handful of books out of the box and slid them onto the bookshelf in the living room. As she unpacked the last of her book collection, she felt as though her home was finally complete, but something was missing this time, and her heart felt empty.

She pulled the next box closer and cut the tape. Bending back the flaps, she lifted Chris's baby book reverently out of the box and smoothed her hand over the pale blue cover. The first pictures were of Chris in her arms—a tiny infant, bundled up in a white blanket. One little hand poked out, and the round dome of his bald head. In the photo, Rachel was looking down at him with a look a sheer wonder on her face.

I had no idea what to expect, she thought with a hint of melancholy.

The next few photos showed her late husband holding Chris, beaming proudly. As she turned the pages, Chris got older. He had his first bath. He met the grandparents in that cross-eyed, confused way that newborns had. He got propped up with teddy bears and slurped at bottles that he learned to hold by himself. He sat up. He crawled. He sprouted his first tooth. Every moment was documented with love and intricate attention to all his little milestones. She pulled the Polaroid picture of Matt holding the newfound Chris in his arms from her pocket.

Matt's eyes looked soft, and Chris snuggled into his neck in the same way she remembered he used to do with her. He looked safe in those muscular arms. He looked cared for, and she felt a wave of gratitude that God had provided someone to cradle her child before she even knew he existed.

What was it about this big firefighter who kept swooping into their life right when they needed rescuing the most?

She tucked the photo into the front of the album, closed it gently and put the album in its place on the bottom shelf.

An image of Matt rose in her mind—Matt in his firefighting suit, dashing into that house after the boy he thought was inside… She'd never seen another man willing to do something like that for her son before, not since Ed. And she'd never met a man who made her feel the way she did right now, either.

And you sent him away, she reminded herself bitterly.

She had been afraid to come in second to the job, but when a man ran into a burning building after your child, it was hard to feel like anything but his top priority. She was afraid to fall in love and then lose him as she had done with Ed, yet wasn't she losing him right this very moment? And hadn't she already fallen in love with him?

Chris had gotten attached, too, and while she'd been so focused on protecting Chris from any more pain in his young life, she was blocking them both from a happy life with a good man—a man she loved.

"Father," she prayed aloud, "have I made a mistake?"

It sure felt like it, but feelings weren't always reliable, either. The job had come first, and while she could understand why, it didn't change facts. He was signing those papers—he'd made his choice long before she'd ever stepped foot in Haggerston. Everything was happening according to plan, even if that plan hurt right now.

The tears she'd been holding back all morning finally spilled onto her cheeks and she covered her face with her hands, her shoulders shaking as sobs overtook her body. A mom needed to be strong for her child, but right now she needed to lean into the invisible arms of her Father and let Him be the strong one. She might be a woman and no longer a hopeful girl, but she'd fallen in love with the tall firefighter in spite of her best efforts, and a broken heart still felt the same.

Mr. Bernard sat down in the visitor chair opposite Matt's desk, a satisfied smile on his face.

"Congratulations, Matthew," Mr. Bernard said. "It was a unanimous vote. We'd like to welcome you to South Maitland's fire department." The older man shook Matt's hand warmly. "How does it feel?"

"Well, I've worked toward this for years, sir," Matt said frankly.

"It's a huge accomplishment, son," Mr. Bernard replied. "You'll be the youngest fire chief I've ever encountered, and that's to your credit. You were more qualified than applicants twenty years your senior. You've certainly worked for this."

"I'm looking forward to meeting the team."

"They're excited to meet you, too. In fact, I have a

couple of real-estate agents who have offered you a cut on their fees if you're looking to buy in the area. But first things first."

Matt glanced around his office, and his eyes lit on the corner of his desk. That was the spot he'd always thought he'd put a picture on when he found the right woman to share his life. He'd proudly put a picture there of the two of them beaming into a camera, and now— Why on earth was that thought so sad right now? Did it matter which desk a picture sat on? It wasn't as if this desk was anything special. Public servants had public service desks—gray metal frames with fake wood tops. *Nothing special*, he told himself. *Pull it together.*

"—don't you think?" Mr. Bernard was saying.

"I'm sorry, sir. I got distracted for a second and missed that."

"I was saying that now would be a good time to sign those papers," the older man repeated, pulling his briefcase up to his lap and flicking open the clasps. "I have to say, the hiring board will be very pleased when I call to say that we've tied this up."

South Maitland was a friendly and beautiful community, located in the center of farm country. Matt had no doubt that he'd enjoy living in that area a lot, and he'd been toying with the idea of buying an acreage—a little more space to spread out. He'd been mentally planning this move for months, yet the excitement of this moment had dried up.

I should be happier, he told himself, as if a mental lecture on the subject would make a difference.

"I think we've talked about all the clauses in your contract," Mr. Bernard said. "Did you have any concerns about it?"

Matt let out a long breath, focusing his thoughts on the contract that lay before him on the desktop. "No, I think it's quite fair. We hammered out that issue with pension, so I think that covered my concerns."

"Excellent." Mr. Bernard shot him a smile and pulled out a pen, clicking it open. "Then all that remains is a signature."

Matt took the pen. It was heavy, perfectly weighted and balanced in his fingers at a satisfying angle.

Lord, I've worked for this and prayed for this. I'm finally getting the fire chief position. This is Your plan for me, isn't it?

He flipped through the pages, initialing in the boxes next to each clause, and when he got to the end, he eyed the bottom line.

"One more John Hancock," Mr. Bernard said, "and I owe you a celebratory dinner, Chief."

Rachel sat on the edge of Chris's bed and looked down at the train track the boy had concocted over the past half hour. The wooden tracks started at one end of the room and looped their way over to the other, a town of toy buildings and block houses populating the entire length. It was impressive and she attempted to show some enthusiasm for his work.

"This is a great town. You've been working hard."

"Yeah." Chris pulled his train slowly over a bridge, then muttered in frustration as it collapsed. "Man, it always does that…"

Rachel slipped off the edge of his bed and sank to the floor next to him. "Sweetie, I wanted to talk to you about something."

"What?" Chris asked, turning his large blue eyes onto her. "Am I in trouble again?"

"No…" She put a hand over his. "Things have been hard lately, haven't they?"

"Yeah." His voice was so soft that she had to lean closer to catch his response.

"What happened at school last year, son? Were the kids teasing you like that boy did here?"

Chris nodded. "I just got so mad."

"How come the teachers didn't notice?" she asked. "They were watching. I asked them to keep an eye out for what was happening."

"I don't know." He shrugged. "It was on the bus."

"Who was the worst?" she asked.

"Virgil."

The fights—the constant fights with those other boys… She'd suspected that there was more to it, but no one would say a word and she was left reprimanding her son for hitting others. Virgil was the principal's son, and suddenly it all fell into place. The teacher had been blaming Chris because she didn't want to point the finger at her boss's son. Tears rose inside her chest.

"And the fire…the one at our old house…"

He was silent for a long moment, and she thought he might not answer her. Finally he looked up into her face, his blue eyes brimming with tears. "I did that."

"But why?" she whispered.

"I was mad." He shrugged weakly.

"Are you still mad?"

"No." His eyes brightened and he dug his heel into the carpet. "I've got Mr. Bailey now, and he can stop the kids from teasing me, so it'll be okay."

Rachel closed her eyes for a moment, summoning

up strength. Was Matt really the one to make her little boy feel strong again? She'd hoped that their friendship would help, and now she'd have to break the hardest news possible. "I wanted to talk to you about Mr. Bailey, too. He's going to be moving away."

"Why?" Chris slapped the bridge down and dashed at the tears that spilled down his cheeks. "That's not fair!"

"He got a job in a different town across the state. So he has to move there."

"He can't just go! He's not supposed to just go away," Chris protested. "Who will make the mean kids stop being mean to me now?"

"I will."

"But you don't know how."

She sighed, the old sadness welling up inside her. "I'll always be here for you, Chris. I'm your mom—we stick together, and we help each other. Always. This is your home and I will hold on to you with all my strength for as long as I live. I don't know exactly how to fix this now, but I'll find the answers. I promise. Mr. Bailey is our friend, and sometimes friends move away, but you can count on me, son."

"But I don't want him to go." He rubbed the tears off his cheeks with the palms of his hands. "I told Mr. Bailey that he couldn't be your boyfriend. Is that why he's going?"

"No." She smiled in spite of it all. "That's not the reason. It isn't because of you."

"But if he was your boyfriend, would he stay?" Chris pressed.

"It doesn't work that way, sweetie," she replied quietly. "Sometimes things get complicated between grown-ups who care about each other a lot."

Chris stood up and wandered over to his open window. He looked down into the yard, his small shoulders drooping. He looked so small, so fragile, and Rachel sent up a prayer, as she always did, that God would protect her little boy. Would Chris be able to face the next school year without his firefighter? He'd have to, and she'd just have to be tougher than ever to stand up for her son.

"Can I talk to him now?" Chris asked, looking back at her.

"Not now," she said. "He's busy now."

The sadness welled up higher inside her heart, and she blinked back the tears. She'd miss Matt, too—more than she'd ever admit to her little boy.

"No, he isn't," Chris countered.

"Chris, please don't argue with me," she said more firmly. "Maybe we can call tomorrow."

"But he's right down there." Chris turned back to the window and peered down. "Hi, Mr. Bailey!"

Rachel blinked and stood up, moving over to the window to look down over the top of her son's head. Matt's truck was parked in the driveway, and he stood beside it, his head tipped back as he looked up at them. He shaded his eyes with one hand, his biceps straining against his shirt. His blue eyes sparkled and he shot her a grin.

"Matt?" She pressed down the surge of relief to see him again so soon and pushed the window farther open. "What are you doing here? I thought you were signing those papers."

"I was. I came back."

His reply was so matter-of-fact. She blinked and pulled away from the window.

"All right, Chris, let's go down and say hello."

Chris scampered ahead of her down the staircase and

flung open the front door before she even had a chance to touch it. Chris crossed the grass and stared accusingly at Matt, crossing his small arms over his chest.

"You're leaving," Chris declared.

"Actually I wanted to talk to your mom about that," he said. "Can you give us a minute, kiddo?"

"You can't go," Chris said, not to be discouraged. "I need you to stay here. You have to help me with the kids at school."

"I will help you with the kids at school," Matt said, squatting down to his level. "I promise, okay?"

"Okay," the boy reluctantly agreed.

Matt rose to his feet and shot Rachel a smile. "Hi."

"What are you doing here?" she asked breathlessly.

"Hey." His tone was low and deep, and he stepped closer so that the warmth of his chest emanated against her. "I didn't sign the papers."

"You didn't?" She gaped up at him. "Why not?"

"Because I couldn't bring myself to do it. I'm in love with you. I can't just leave town and walk away." His gaze flickered toward Chris, then back to her eyes. "From either of you."

"You—" She cleared her throat. "You love me?"

"Heart and soul, babe." He moved a strand of hair away from her face. "Do you love me?"

She nodded, emotion rising in her throat. "Of course I love you. But if it isn't this job, it will be another one—"

"No." He shook his head. "I made my peace with a few things at the graveyard today, and I'm not going anywhere. I'm staying here in Haggerston."

"Even if nothing happens between you and me?" she asked, a teasing smile coming to her lips. She didn't mean a word of that. She was too grateful to see him again to even consider pushing him away again.

He stepped closer, his forehead gently touching hers, and he chuckled. "I'll just keep trying."

Rachel laughed and pulled away, heat rising in her cheeks. "So I suppose we could see how things go…"

"I want to marry you," he replied, tugging her back. "I want to be together, a family, for the rest of my life. I love you. I want to take care of you and wake up to you. I want to raise Chris with you and make sure that no one ever pushes him around again. I just can't see myself happy anywhere, unless I've got you with me. And you need to be here for Chris, and that means I stay."

"You're putting us first?" she asked, tears misting her eyes.

"You'll always be first in my heart. You know what the job entails, and it demands a lot, but I can promise you one thing—I'll never turn off my phone. I'll always take your call." He paused and gave her a roguish grin. "Unless I'm actually inside a burning building, of course…"

Rachel laughed softly. "It sounds like a good deal."

"So what do you say? Will you marry me?"

She nodded, words stuck in her throat. She could feel the beat of his heart against her hands, and his warm gaze pulled her in. Matt leaned down and pressed his lips gently against hers. She slid closer into his strong arms, the scent of his aftershave filling her up. Pulling back, he looked down into her face with a grin.

"That was a yes, right?" he clarified.

"Yes!" She laughed, and he kissed her again.

When he finally pulled back, she found herself breathless and a little weak-kneed. She looked over to find Chris staring up at them, his small face screwed up into an expression of "ick."

"Ew," he said reproachfully.

"Chris, Mr. Bailey is going to stay after all, and I think we have something to talk to you about." She glanced up at Matt, and the big firefighter shot her a grin.

"We also have a ring to shop for," he said softly, pulling her hand into his. "And wedding plans to make."

"You could also buy me ice cream," Chris suggested helpfully, and Matt laughed, throwing an arm around his shoulders.

"Hop up in the truck, Chris," he said. "Ice cream it is."

Epilogue

The little parking lot for Peace Hills Christian Church was packed, and all along the gravel road, cars parked on either side. The small copses that sprang up out of the rolling fields shone orange and crimson in all their autumn glory. The mown fields stretched out like gold, huge round bales of hay dotting the landscape around the little white church, freshly painted during a community work bee. It was high time the church was painted again, everybody said, especially for a wedding.

Chris, dressed in a little tuxedo, sat on the steps to the church, staring stoically out at the fields while muffled organ music filtered out from inside the church. Rachel sat next to him, her ivory gown billowing out around her, her veil pushed back over her dark hair and fluttering in the cool breeze.

The school year was off to a successful start. Chris hadn't been in a fight yet, and his teacher had already told Matt and Rachel a few times what a smart kid he was and how impressed she was with his maturity. He'd been teased once or twice, but he'd come home and told his mother about it right away, and Matt had gone in to have a word with the principal, and the teasing stopped. Matt wouldn't have accepted anything less. He was respected in this town, and his word went a long way.

The teachers were taking the bullying seriously, and they were already planning school-wide adoption education to clear up some of the misconceptions. He and Rachel were determined to find the support they needed as parents—parents! He never thought he'd step into fatherhood so easily, but he had.

Matt crouched down in front of them where they sat on the wooden steps of the church. The forlorn look on Chris's face made the inside of his chest ache. This boy had been through enough, and with the wedding drawing closer, Matt had been afraid of this happening.

"Are you two okay?" Matt asked. Rachel shot him a grateful smile. She reached out and took his hand.

Chris looked miserably over at Matt. "No."

"What's wrong, Chris?"

"I don't think I want you to marry my mom, after all."

Matt sighed and leaned his elbows onto his knees. The three of them sat in silence for a couple of minutes, watching the mowers in the distance creeping over the fields. Warm autumn sunlight poured over their shoulders, and a chill in the air cooled them just as quickly.

"What made you change your mind, kiddo?"

"I dunno."

"You're used to being your mom's main guy, aren't you?" he asked.

"I can take care of my mom," Chris replied, his voice low.

"I know. And you've done a good job of that," Matt said. "So I guess you and I should probably talk about this man-to-man, right?"

Chris looked up, surprise registering in his blue eyes. "Yeah, man-to-man."

Rachel looked curiously between them. "Do you need some privacy for this?"

"No, that's okay," Matt said. "I can say this stuff in front of you, gorgeous."

Chris made a face and Matt chuckled.

"Okay, Chris, I'm going to say it straight. I love your mom a lot, but I see that I need to make a deal with you."

"I don't need toys or anything," the boy retorted reproachfully.

"That wouldn't be a deal man-to-man," Matt said frankly. "This is a grown-up deal."

"Okay…" Chris eyed him speculatively.

"I'm going to make you a promise, Chris. I promise that I'll never hurt your mom. I'll never make her cry, and I'll do everything I can to make her as happy as I possibly can. And I mean that. That's a solemn promise."

Rachel's dark gaze met his, her soft lips turning up into a misty smile.

Chris's lip trembled. "But what about me?"

"I'll always need you, sweetheart," Rachel said, pulling the boy against her. "Always."

"Here's the thing, kiddo," Matt said quietly. "You and your mom are a family because when she adopted you, she chose you to be her son. It doesn't matter how old you get, you'll always be her son. And now your mom and I are getting married because we chose each other. Choosing is what makes a family, Chris. I'm not just choosing your mom. I'm choosing you, too."

Chris sat in silence for a long moment, and then he turned and looked up at Matt quizzically. "You're choosing me?"

"Absolutely. I'm choosing you to be my kid. And your mom to be my wife." His gaze flickered toward his beautiful bride. "And when I marry your mom, I'm promising both of you that I'll be here for you for the rest of our lives. We'll be a forever family. I'm going to take care of you both, provide for you, look out for you, and even if I can't come home some nights because I have to be in the fire station, you can call me and I'll always pick up, no matter the time. That's a promise, kiddo. And you can bank on it. It's a promise I'm making inside a *church*."

Chris looked back at the church doors, clearly impressed with the weight of those words. Finally he nodded. "Okay."

"Okay." Matt rose to his feet. "So, can we go in now and make this official?"

Chris nodded, and Rachel rose to her feet. The wind pushed against her gown, nudging and billowing the rustling ivory material. As she brushed her veil back, her dark waves shining in the autumn sunlight, Matt was struck anew with a wave of overpowering love for this woman. He watched in protective admiration as Rachel and Chris went up the wooden stairs toward the door, her veil fluttering out behind her, and the boy holding tight to her hand. He'd never forget this moment or this image in his mind. This would be the moment he told their grandchildren about—the moment when his life truly began.

"Mr. Bailey?" Chris turned back.

"Yeah?"

"Can I call you Dad?"

A lump rose in Matt's throat and Rachel looked back at him, tears shining in her eyes. He nodded. "I'd really like that, Chris."

Matt jogged up the stairs to catch up with them and pulled open the church door. Rachel leaned into his chest and looked up at him adoringly. He slid an arm around her waist, holding himself back from pulling her into his arms and kissing her quite thoroughly. That would have to wait until the ceremony.

"There you are!" Aunt Louise exclaimed, and just as quickly, she tugged Rachel out of his arms and toward a side room. "Quick, quick!" she ordered. "Matt, you are needed at the front of the church, and, Rachel, your makeup needs just one more touch-up…"

Today, he was making a promise in that little country church, and it was one he would guard for the rest of his life. Today, he would pledge to be hers and start a life as a husband, a father and part of their forever family. "Come on, Chris," he said with a grin. "We'd better get up there."

* * * * *

Dear Reader,

When researching this book, I walked down to our local fire hall, smiled sweetly at the receptionist and asked to speak to someone—anyone, really—about how a fire hall runs. The very kind deputy fire chief cleared his throat from where he stood watching us at the doorway and said, "Can I help you out with something?"

I thought to myself, *I've got to use that in my book. That was fantastic.*

The book was born.

Not only did the deputy chief answer my questions and give me a tour, but he impressed me with his professionalism and won my respect. The firefighters who put their lives on the line to keep our communities safe deserve nothing less.

I hope you've enjoyed this story, and I hope that you'll come by to see me on my Patricia Johns Romance Facebook page and my blog (PatriciaJohnsRomance.com). I love to connect with readers. If you message me, I'll be sure to answer. That's a promise…a novelist's promise, which is significantly less romantic than a firefighter's promise, but it's what I've got.

Each and every one of you is a living, breathing story, and with God that story always has a happy ending! In the meantime, let's stick together, ladies. The plot might thicken, but the ending is a guarantee. Let's build each other up and show the next generation of girls that together is the best way to be.

Patricia Johns

REQUEST YOUR FREE BOOKS!

2 FREE INSPIRATIONAL NOVELS
PLUS 2
FREE
MYSTERY GIFTS

LI15

*Can a widow and widower ever leave their grief in the
past and forge a new future—and a family—together?*

*Read on for a sneak preview of
THE AMISH WIDOW'S SECRET.*

"Wait, before you go. I have an important question to ask
you."

Sarah nodded her head and sat back down.

"I stayed up until late last night, thinking about your
situation and mine. I prayed, and *Gott* kept pushing this
thought at me." He took a deep breath. "I wonder, would
you consider becoming my *frau*?"

Sarah held up her hand, as if to stop his words. "I…"

"Before you speak, let me explain." Mose took another
deep breath. "I know you still love Joseph, just as I still
love my Greta. But I have *kinder* who need a mother to
guide and love them. Now that Joseph's gone and the
farm's being sold, you need a place to call home, people
who care about you, a family. We can join forces and help
each other." He saw a panicked expression forming in her
eyes. "It would only be a marriage of convenience. The
girls need a loving mother and you've already proven you
can be that. What do you say, Sarah Nolt? Will you be
my wife?"

Sarah sat silent, her face turned away. She looked into
Mose's eyes. "You'd do this for me? But…you don't
know me."

"I'd do this for us," Mose corrected, and smiled.

The tips of Sarah's fingers nervously pleated and unpleated a scrap of her skirt. "But we hardly know each other. What would people think? They will say I took advantage of your good nature."

Mose smiled. "So, let them talk. They'd be wrong and we'd know it. I want this marriage for both of us, for the *kinder*. We can't let others decide what is best for our lives. I believe this marriage is *Gott*'s plan for us."

Sarah's face cleared and she seemed to come to a decision. She smoothed out the fabric of her skirt and tidied her hair, then finally took Mose's outstretched hand with a smile. "You're right. This is our life. I accept your proposal, Mose Fisher. I will be your *frau* and your *kinder*'s mother."

Don't miss
THE AMISH WIDOW'S SECRET
by Cheryl Williford,
available June 2015 wherever
Love Inspired® books and ebooks are sold.